MAKE YOU STAY

M.L. BROOME

TerraCotta Dragon Arts

Make You Stay

Copyright © J.E. Soper 2021

All rights reserved.

This book is a work of fiction. References to real people, events, establishments, organizations, or locales are intended only to provide a sense of authenticity and are used fictitiously. Names, characters, dialogue and incidents depicted in this book are products of the author's imagination and are not to be construed as real.

No part of this publication may be reproduced, downloaded, transmitted, decompiled, reverse-engineered, or stored into any information storage and retrieval system, in any form or by any means, whether electronic or mechanical, now known or hereafter invented, without the express written permission of J.E. Soper and TerraCotta Dragon Arts.

Digital Edition AUGUST 2021 ISBN TBA

Print Edition ISBN: TBA

Cover Design

Mallory Crowe

To Astrid, for never ceasing to believe in me and forcing me to believe in myself. When I wanted to quit, you wouldn't hear it and certainly, would never allow it.

Thank you for being my champion, my sounding board, but mostly, my friend.

I am blessed in this world because you are in it.

All the love, today and always.

For what it's worth:
it's never too late or, in my case,
too early to be whoever you want to be.
There's no time limit,
stop whenever you want.
You can change or stay the same,
there are no rules to this thing.
We can make the best or the worst of it.
I hope you make the best of it,
and I hope you see things that startle you.
I hope you feel things you never felt before.
I hope you meet people
with a different point of view.
I hope you life a life you're proud of.
If you find that you're not,
I hope you find the courage to start all over again.

~ F. Scott Fitzgerald

PROLOGUE
CHLOE

The phone slips from my grip, smacking against the floorboards with a thud, but I make no move to retrieve it. Instead, I shift my gaze to the suitcase yawning on my bed, empty save for a box of photos and trinkets. Items I planned to share during my visit now serve as a mocking reminder that my upcoming vacation to Asheville is no longer a vacation.

Some part of me isn't even surprised at this macabre turn of events. It is *my* life, after all, and the gods seem fit to use it as fodder for their twisted senses of humor.

Slinking into the living area, I glare at the lights twinkling around my window, right next to the four-foot artificial tree I insist on putting up every year in my shoebox-sized Manhattan apartment. I'm fully aware it's only November, but I'm one of *those* people who set up for Christmas before Thanksgiving arrives. Despite the latent commercialism, I adore the holiday season—the festivities and chaotic excitement flowing through the city warms my soul even as the northeast winds threaten to freeze me whole.

At least I *did* enjoy the season until the phone call a few moments earlier, which upended my equilibrium.

For the first time in twenty-four years, I planned to spend the Thanksgiving holiday with my mother.

Instead, I'll be attending her funeral.

She never mentioned any upcoming surgery, but I'm hardly surprised. Betsey and I rarely said much to each other. That was the point of this trip—reconnecting and rekindling our relationship, which died out years ago.

No chance of that, now.

The tears threaten to overpower me, clogging any other emotion from reaching the surface as my mind tries to reconcile the unfairness of this situation.

Granted, fairness was never a cornerstone of my life, thanks in part to Betsey. My mother, according to those who knew her when, was an unforgettable spirit. I'll tell you one thing, she was good at forgetting me, but that's a conversation for another time.

A one-sided conversation now.

With a sigh, I drag myself back to the bedroom. No point in wasting time wondering about what might have been.

Might have been is a terrible term, reminding people of all their lost chances and wrong choices.

Better to focus on the present and the task at hand. Namely, rethinking my wardrobe for this trip.

Originally, I planned on staying a few weeks, but now, it's anyone's guess. Her lawyer informed me that Betsey left me everything, not that I know what *everything* entails. I have the task of sorting her estate and putting up for sale the home I now own in the mountains of North Carolina.

The only saving grace in this situation? Betsey pre-planned

her funeral, down to the last detail. She also paid for everything in advance, not that money is a problem. I make plenty of green as a freelance writer and can more than afford her burial costs.

The bigger issue? I don't know Betsey, except on a superficial level. Things that a daughter should know—her favorite color, food, and song—are all mysteries to me. To be fair, she doesn't know mine either.

Didn't know mine.

This whole past tense, when referring to Betsey, is going to take some getting used to, although she never was a constant in my life. Now that chance has flown away like autumn leaves in a November breeze.

Per her lawyer, who claims to have known Betsey for decades, she was a spitfire, and her memorial service will reflect that vibrant energy. At least I don't have to bumble my way through a generic service, which is the best I can offer with my limited knowledge. How do you plan a memorial for a woman who's noticeably absent from your memories?

Thankfully for me, I don't.

Now all I have to do is fly to Asheville a few days earlier than originally planned.

How hard can it be? I live in Manhattan. Our airports carry thousands of passengers all around the world, every day.

Two hours and a martini later, I have my answer. I also have a flight to Asheville, with a three-hour layover in Virginia. Simple enough, especially for someone who has traveled around the globe.

The caveat? Mother nature is behaving like an uncooperative bitch. The meteorologists are calling for an unseasonably early snowstorm in the Appalachians on the same day I'm scheduled to fly out.

Per the airline reservation attendant, they're hoping to beat the storm, but, and I'm quoting here, it's anyone's guess how it will turn out.

Not instilling great confidence with that statement, and judging by my recent run of luck, I don't stand a chance for things to go smoothly.

CHAPTER 1

AIDAN

"Look who finally decided to show up," I mutter under my breath, earning a side-eye glare from my ex-wife Enid.

"Aidan," she hisses over the heads of our two youngest daughters.

With a scoff, I toss up my hands. "I'm just saying. What could be more important than arriving on time to your mother's funeral?"

No joke.

Who arrives late to their mother's funeral?

Chloe Strickland, apparently.

I watch her scurry in through the church doors, nearly ten minutes after the service began, settling into a seat in the back corner.

We've never met—officially—but I'd know the woman anywhere. Her photos litter the walls and fireplace mantle of Betsey's home, even though I'm well aware, per Betsey's own admission, that Chloe never set foot in the farmhouse.

Until today.

I get it. Some folks aren't close with their parents. Hell, I barely spoke to my old man for years. But my old man was a drunk and a mean one at that. After he beat my ass for the umpteenth time over something as arbitrary as the color of the sky, I'd had enough. I left and never looked back.

Betsey is nothing like my old man. She was funny and outgoing, with a laugh that danced across your eardrums. She was more than my neighbor. Over the last five years, she'd become one of my closest friends and a grandmother figure to my daughters. The concept of someone not loving Betsey is like a child hating Santa Claus—it's not normal.

I don't know Chloe's reason for abandoning her mother, although I've no doubt it's utterly selfish in nature. Likely, the bright lights of the big city blinded her to what matters in life.

Betsey spoke about Chloe quite often and how she longed for a closer relationship with her only child. She was desperate to play matchmaker, exclaiming how she planned on setting us up when her daughter arrived for a visit. It didn't matter how many times I told her I wasn't interested in that plan because Betsey wouldn't take no for an answer.

Chloe is undoubtedly beautiful, far and away prettier than her pictures. She bears a strong resemblance to Betsey when she was younger—long dark hair, wide dark eyes, and a killer body.

Betsey may have been pushing sixty-five, but she took care of herself. Prided herself on her appearance. She was a dancer in her younger days, a self-proclaimed gypsy and free spirit. Maybe that's why she seemed timeless.

And Chloe? She's more stunning than her mother, even though I want nothing to do with the woman.

She didn't care enough about my dear friend to be in her life. Now, I'll ensure Chloe is never a part of mine.

The minister signals to me, and I stand, running a hand down the length of my beard. Betsey pre-planned her funeral, complete with the people she wanted to speak.

Imagine my surprise when *I* was one of those people... and Chloe wasn't.

Like I said, her daughter is not normal. She's no doubt in town to lay claim to her inheritance. It's sickening how people emerge from the shadows when someone dies, like cockroaches when you turn out the light.

I'll bet there are a ton of cockroaches in New York City.

Sighing, I will my anger down. There's a time and place for that emotion, but it isn't here.

Walking to the podium, I pull the folded paper from my pocket, my green eyes scanning the crowd. A full house, full of people Betsey called family.

Ironic how the only bloodline link sits in the back corner, her gaze fixed on me, her face belying any emotion. I guess the cold has frozen the woman's heart solid.

"Afternoon, folks. As I look around the room, I see so many familiar faces. People who loved Betsey and who she loved in return. I was lucky to call her not only my neighbor but my friend. Not that I had much choice in the matter. She charmed my daughters immediately with tales of magical lands. It was only a matter of time before she charmed me, as well."

My gaze narrows, its laser focus on Chloe. I hope she feels the intensity of my glare. "I pity those people who didn't take the time to know Betsey Strickland. Their loss, really, but most definitely my gain. Sometimes you don't know what you have until it's gone. In my case, I know exactly how precious that woman was to me. In typical Betsey fashion, she arranged a luncheon for all of us, complete with the requisite shot of Irish whiskey. I hope you're thirsty, folks, because Betsey always threw one hell of a party." Motioning to the ceiling, I blink back tears, willing myself to make it through the remainder of the speech. "Here's to you, Bets. Thanks for the memories."

The strains of Betsey's favorite song drift over the church speakers, and I bite back a laugh. A true testament to the power of Betsey Strickland's charm, finagling the local preacher to play Prince instead of a standard hymn.

Chloe nods in my direction, but I turn away, my temper threatening to get the better of me.

Don't thank me for loving your mother. Ask yourself why you didn't.

I wish I had a mother like Betsey, though I suppose these last few years, I did. I grew up in a funhouse of terrors, with a drunkard father and a mother too beaten down to care anymore. There wasn't any parental influence, so I raised myself before running away to get married and start my own family.

I had one goal for my kids. They would know, beyond a shadow of a doubt, that their old man put them first.

Always.

"What was that?" Enid mutters, switching seats with our middle child, Emily, to sit next to me.

"What? Betsey requested I say a few words. I had *nothing* to do with the Prince song."

"Not that. Your pointed barbs at Betsey's daughter."

"I never mentioned her daughter."

My ex-wife knows me far too well to buy that load of crap. "Maybe not by name, but this whole church got your innuendo. Don't be an asshole."

"Language, Mom." This warning comes from our youngest daughter, Mia, as she smiles up at me with a gap-filled grin. Mia is six going on thirty. She has a neighborhood lemonade stand that pulls in thousands per summer. I'm only thankful lemonade is legal. She decided a few months ago that both her mom and dad cursed too much, so she started a curse jar, charging us every time we dared to cross her path.

At the rate we're going, the kid will be able to afford a Mercedes by the new year.

"Your father deserved it," Enid argues, huffing out a sigh of resignation as she glances at her husband. "Jeff, can you give Mia a dollar, please?"

Jeff smirks, pulling out his wallet. "I'm going to start adding interest to these bailouts."

"I'll make it up to you in other ways."

I close my eyes, shaking my head at the bevy of information I did *not* need. Natalie, my oldest at sixteen, agrees, coughing in disgust at Enid's flirtatious banter with her husband.

Some people might find it odd how close Enid and I are after our divorce. I find it strange how you can hate someone you once loved more than life. And I still love Enid, just not in that way. We share three daughters—beautiful terrors that we adore. When we split, we realized divorce didn't have to be messy. That's a choice.

We chose to be classy and gracious, giving each other the space and support we needed to begin a new life path. Funnily enough, we discovered we were better as friends, something we might have realized years ago if Enid didn't get pregnant at twenty-two.

When Enid met Jeff, she was terrified of my reaction, but I put her mind at ease. Jeff is a hell of a good guy, and he loves our daughters. He also loves Enid. The two of us got along immediately, and by the end of our first beer, we were buddies.

Still are to this day.

We're family, and no matter how odd the pieces fit, they still do.

Unlike Chloe, who walked away from her family.

I sure hope she's happy with her decision.

THE GIRLS AND I RETURN HOME A FEW HOURS LATER. Despite Betsey's wish for an all-night party, Mother Nature has other ideas. Namely, a second helping of the snow we got earlier in the week.

Asheville gets its fair share of the white stuff, but the weather has been particularly generous this year. Emily loves it, always eager to don her snow gear and spend hours building snowmen and forts.

That is, until I haul out the snowblower, destroying her eleven-year-old dreams. She can't comprehend why I prefer a concrete driveway to a snow-covered one.

One day, she will.

I have the girls tonight, so the four of us pile into the living room, ready to watch a movie. Tonight is Emily's choice, and I never know what random film she's going to request. No joke. One time she selected *Tora Tora Tora*—I have no clue how she even *heard* of that wartime movie.

Unlike her older sister, Natalie, who's popular and trendy, and her younger sister, Mia, who's building an empire before the age of ten, Emily is quiet. Studious. Her eyes pierce through your skin and stare straight into your soul.

She's my best mate on this planet, and her sisters never let her forget it.

"What's your pick, kid?" I ask, ruffling Emily's hair.

"Do you think we should ask Chloe if she wants to join us?"

My daughter's question startles me, my eyes widening in shock. "Why?"

Emily shrugs, staring at the floor. "She just lost her mom, and she's all alone next door."

"She's fine," I mutter, refusing to feel sympathy for the woman who couldn't manage to visit her mother when she was on *this* side of the dirt.

"I spoke with her at the restaurant," Natalie pipes in, sitting cross-legged on the floor as she braids Mia's hair. "She's really nice. Funny, just like Betsey."

"She's nothing like Betsey." I refuse to budge an inch where this woman is concerned. Maybe she didn't give a damn about Betsey, but I did.

"How would you know, Dad? You didn't even speak to her," Natalie retorts, fixing me with her green gaze.

I hate how this girl always calls me on the carpet.

Just like her mother.

"Can we watch a movie?" Mia asks, harrumphing out her impatience.

"That's the best idea I've heard in a while." Leave it to my six-year-old to throw her dad a lifeline.

Anything to get us off the topic of Chloe Strickland.

That is one woman I have no desire to discuss.

Ever.

All I can hope is that by some magic, she up and disappears in the middle of the night, never to be seen again.

CHAPTER 2
CHLOE

It's after nine when I finally cave to the cold, my teeth chattering even under the pile of blankets. I'm a native New Yorker and used to frigid temperatures, but my heat operated via a thermostat, not some mammoth stove that looked ready to explode.

I may be a chickenshit, but I wasn't tempting fate after the day I had yesterday. It's bad enough I barely made the funeral service after missing every turn and almost sliding off the side of a mountain en route to Asheville.

So, after the party Betsey had organized to celebrate her life, I returned to her house—*my* house now, at least according to the will.

Then I downed a shot of vodka and crawled into bed in the guest room.

I suppose I figured the house would remain a certain temperature, what with insulation and such.

It did, too. The same temperature as an igloo. Possibly a few degrees lower.

After shooting the stove a glare, I pad past it into the kitchen. At least I can figure out how to work the coffeemaker. Thank God for small favors.

The sheer amount of space around me is shocking after a lifetime in Manhattan. My apartment is tiny, but it's in a highly desirable area of Tribeca. I'm close to everything. The pulse of humanity is right outside my door.

Here, even with ample room, I feel like a caged animal.

Hell, I can't even figure out how to work the stove, and I'm sure my new neighbor won't offer any assistance. It was impossible to miss his glare or the cold vibes he tossed in my direction at Betsey's funeral.

I get it. To these people, I'm an outsider. A damn Yankee. A prissy and highfaluting woman from the big city come down here to flaunt my life in their faces.

They couldn't be more wrong. I'm actually falling apart, even though I have no plan on letting *them* know that fact.

Not that they'd care, regardless. My welcome was chillier than the interior of this house.

No matter what they think about me, or my Yankee lifestyle, I didn't ask for this or for the first steps into my mother's home to be after we lowered her body into the ground. Life happens. Shit happens.

Often at the same time.

Pulling the blanket tighter around my shoulders, I search the cabinets for some creamer or sugar. None to be found.

Black coffee, it is.

"It's freezing in here."

I jump at the unexpected voice, believing for a second that my mother's ghost has returned from the grave.

Instead, I see Natalie from next door in my hallway. She's the oldest of the three girls and was apparently very close with Betsey. At sixteen, she's also willowy and tall, with bright green eyes sparkling with mischief.

She's going to be a heartbreaker one day.

"It's beyond freezing. I don't know how to work the woodstove."

"I'll get it." She does, too. Within two minutes, the sucker is glowing orange. "There, it should warm the place up within an hour. You can close some doors to the spare rooms. It will keep the heat centralized."

"Thank you." Motioning to the coffeepot, I offer her a mug. "Are you allowed to drink coffee?"

Natalie laughs, shaking her head. "I don't need the caffeine. I'm too high-strung already." She fingers some of the photos I spread across the kitchen table the night before. "These are great. I remember Betsey showed me some of these."

A swell of resentment floods my body. How nice for Natalie, knowing my mother's history. Betsey never showed me *anything*. Swallowing back my anger with a gulp of coffee, I force a smile. "Did she? I'd love to hear the stories."

"Don't you know them?"

"No. Betsey wasn't in my life for many years."

"How come?"

"That's a good question, Natalie." The words slip out before I can grab them back. "I'm not entirely sure. I guess I wasn't what she wanted."

Natalie cocks her head, a look of confusion on her face. "You're her daughter. You have to love your kids."

"If only that were the truth because sadly, many parents *don't* love their kids. Although your parents obviously adore you girls. Besides, I know Betsey loved me, in her way."

"She always said she did, even though she never saw you." Natalie picks up a black-and-white photo of Betsey in a dance costume. "I remember this story. This was when a sheik invited her to perform for him. Only dancing, no sex."

I choke at her brash comment. "She told you that?"

"She did. I'm sure she embellished, but that's what you do with a good story, right?" Plopping down at the table, she crosses her legs under her. "I can help you go through them if you like."

The loneliness clawing at my heart threatens to rip me apart at her kind offer. Mainly because they're the *only* kind words I've heard since I arrived in Asheville, with the exception of Natalie's younger sister, Emily. Oh, people patted my arm and forced a smile for me yesterday, but none of them cared how I felt.

Why should they? I'm nothing to them. Apparently, Betsey was everything.

A memorable woman that I don't remember.

"I would like that—" Someone pounds at the door, and I startle again. "This house sure sees a lot of traffic."

"Probably my dad," Natalie mutters. "I'm in the kitchen."

My body stiffens the moment Aidan walks into the room, moving with an authoritative gait, his face stern. At least, I *think* it's stern. Impossible to tell with the beard covering half his face and stretching down to the middle of his chest.

That is one look I never understood.

"Natalie, get in the car. We're going to be late." He juts his chin in my direction. "She'll be out of your way in a second."

"She's fine. Actually, she was a tremendous help. I didn't know how to work the stove—"

"You don't know how to work a stove? What do you use in Manhattan?"

My fingers tighten around my mug, shocked by his biting

remark. What crawled up his ass and died? Hell, I didn't tell him to wear the dead animal on his face. That was entirely his decision.

"I live in an apartment building that has a boiler and a maintenance crew."

"Of course, you do."

"Dad, leave her alone," Natalie interjects, glaring at her father.

"Go wait in the car," Aidan repeats, holding his ground until the front door closes. "I'll tell Natalie to keep her distance."

"She's more than welcome here. Anytime."

"Won't that cramp your big city style?"

And just like that, my big city *temper* shows up to the party. "Contrary to what *you* believe, living in a city doesn't mean I'm without manners or morals. There are actually very nice people in Manhattan."

"Sure, there are."

"Truth is, I've met far more hostile individuals down here in North Carolina."

"Is that comment pointed in a specific direction?" His eyes flash at me, but I'm not backing down.

"Yes. Yours. I don't know why you hate me, Aidan. I have done nothing."

"Exactly."

"What the hell does that mean?"

Aidan takes a step closer, pointing an accusatory finger in my direction. "Betsy was one of the sweetest women I've ever known. She loved everyone, and everyone loved her, except for her daughter, who was noticeably absent right up until her funeral. Too busy living your glamorous life in New York to kowtow to your mother, huh?"

This self-righteous son of a bitch. "The Betsey you knew and the one I knew are two different women. You're correct that my relationship with my mother was strained, but I will not own all the blame for it."

"How can you not? She was right here, day after day. Look around you! There are photos of you everywhere."

I storm into the back room, motioning to the framed photos on the wall. "Look closer, Aidan. Do you notice she isn't in any of them with me? Why do you suppose that is?" Sucking in a deep breath, I search for my center, but it's nowhere to be found. "I will not do this with you. Think what you want. Tell Natalie what you want. Just leave me alone."

❦

MY FIRST ORDER OF BUSINESS? GETTING THIS HOUSE packed and ready to sell. I need out of North Carolina and fast.

If I thought I was unwelcome before, Aidan solidified it with his biting commentary. The man apparently hates me, and I'm not sure how to handle it.

I've never had a perfect stranger hate me before. God only knows what Betsey told him about me. To be honest, the woman knew very little about me, but the truth is often a minor detail.

As I walk through her century-old farmhouse, my eyes catch on several half-finished construction projects. Wonderful. Now I have to find a contractor to repair… whatever it is she was doing. I don't even know who started the job or if they have any intention of returning.

This is the added bonus of someone dying unexpectedly. There are a billion loose ends everywhere, and now it's the job of someone else—in my case, a virtual stranger—to muddle through the muck and figure it out.

Per Betsey's lawyer, she went in for a minor routine procedure. She fully expected to come out. That's the crux of irony.

Coulda, woulda, shoulda.

I wonder if Aidan would have been so terrible had Betsey survived. Would he have been neighborly and friendly at the holiday gathering or taken me to task over my Yankee upbringing?

Funny, my mother often spoke about how she thought Aidan and I would be a splendid match.

Shows how little the woman knew about me.

I suppose he's good-looking, in a rough-hewn, backwoods kind of way. That beard eats up most of his face, and after his rude comments this morning, I have half a mind to grab the scissors and cut off his pride and joy. Some women love full beards. I'm not one of them.

But I could have overlooked the damn facial hair if the man had mustered a smile in my direction. Since he didn't, I didn't feel the need to be kind in return.

Needless to say, battle lines have been drawn in a war I didn't know I was fighting.

He does have the most intensely beautiful green eyes I've ever seen. Nice hands, too, if we're doling out compliments. Beyond that, Aidan can sod off. Him and his moral high ground.

I throw on my coat with a grunt, determined to find a snow shovel and clear the walks. Mother Nature and her sense of humor—here, the ground is covered while in New York, we're dealing with unseasonably warm temperatures.

I can't wait to go home.

After locating the shovel in the shed and damn near falling on my ass trying to get it out, I trudge through the snow, intent on the task at hand.

"My Dad does that," a soft voice says to my right. Glancing

up, I spy Emily, Aidan's middle daughter, who stuck to my side like glue yesterday.

In truth, she was the only one who did. She even held my hand at the restaurant after finding me huddled alone in a corner.

Now, she's in the middle of building a snow castle or something to that effect.

"I like your snow house."

"It's a fort. Want me to get Dad?"

Please, God, don't do that.

I shake my head. "I've got it. It's good exercise."

"Do you get snow in New York?"

"Tons of it, but I don't have a driveway to shovel."

Her eyes widen with curiosity. "Where do you park your car?"

"I don't have a car. I live in the city, and I take the subway. It's an underground train. Have you ever been to New York?"

"No. Ms. Strickland used to talk about the big city lights, but she liked it better here in Asheville."

That's the understatement of the century.

I can tell Emily wants to continue talking, but I have to put space between us. It doesn't matter that Aidan's girls are smart and funny or that I adore children. Their father has made it abundantly clear he wants me nowhere near them. It's as though I have some disease he's afraid they'll catch, turning them *all* into damn Yankees.

So, no matter how unfair or unwarranted his opinion of me, I must respect his wishes.

It was much the same situation with Henry and Jeff, my ex-boyfriend's sons. I helped raise them for the better part of five years, but one day Charlie came home to let me know that his ex-wife was back in town and looking for a reconciliation.

It didn't matter that she hadn't seen the boys in years. She was in while he kicked me to the curb, asking that I not contact the boys as it would be too confusing for them.

It was sure as hell confusing for *me*.

But I respected Charlie's wishes then, and I'll respect Aidan's now.

Respect is a funny thing. It's expected but rarely earned. Should be the other way around.

"Did you get a letter?" Emily inquires, moving closer to my side.

My brows knit. "A letter?"

"From Ms. Strickland. Your mom."

"No. Did you?"

Emily nods, pulling it from her pocket. "She wrote one for each of us. Me and my sisters. She liked writing letters and telling stories. You would have liked her."

Those words, spoken by an eleven-year-old girl, break me, and the tears I've held back finally have their due. I'm sure I *would* have liked Betsey if I had the chance to know her as they did.

Emily, seeing my tears, rushes over, grasping me in a hug about the waist. "Don't cry, Chloe. I'll tell you her stories."

"I'd like that," I manage, wiping my eyes as I see Aidan standing at his front door, glaring in our direction.

So much for that respect I mentioned earlier.

"You'd better go finish that fort. I have to get busy shoveling."

Emily glances over her shoulder before nodding. Seems she understands the circumstances and the hostile energy emanating from her father toward me. "I'll see you soon, Chloe, and I'll send Dad out to help you."

Before I can argue her statement, she bounds inside.

Wonderful, now he'll no doubt be on my doorstep within the hour, even more caustic than before as he accuses me of buttering up his children.

Tossing down the shovel, I scurry inside to hide, praying I won't have to battle Aidan a second time this morning.

CHAPTER 3
AIDAN

"Why were you hugging her?" I ask Emily as she bounds through the front door.

"She needed a hug." My middle child shrugs at me as if I've lost my mind for asking such a question.

"Yeah, Dad, you could try being nice to Chloe." Natalie slides into a chair at the kitchen table, wearing her sternest expression.

Are they kidding me?

"She doesn't deserve it. That woman abandoned her mother."

"Not according to the letter," comes Natalie's enigmatic reply.

"What letter?"

My eldest pulls a piece of paper from her purse, sliding it across the table. "Betsey sent each of us one."

Grabbing the paper, I pull it open, curious what my friend wanted to say to my children. Especially if it involves Chloe in some way.

Dear Nat,

I love you like a granddaughter. All our talks, stories, and laughs. You are a bright light, much like my own daughter.

You need to know the whole truth of my daughter, as it weighs heavily on my mind. You often asked, with that direct manner so like your father, why Chloe was noticeably absent. Never a part of my life.

The truth is, I wasn't a part of her life. I left her when she was only twelve.

My selfish heart had dreams beyond my family. Dreams of dancing in the mountains that called me home.

My husband's life and work were in New York, but our marriage was nothing more than a paper contract at that point. My fault, not his. He knew I desired my freedom, so he let me go, refusing to cage me like a bird.

And I flew, leaving them both behind. I left Chloe in a quest to find myself.

We didn't speak for years. She was angry, and rightfully so. Hurt that her mother didn't care enough to stick around. Her father raised her right, and Chloe grew into a beautiful and successful woman.

A woman I don't know.

That is my biggest regret. I can't wait for Thanksgiving to arrive. I hope to rekindle the love I never lost for my daughter and show her—finally—that the mother who walked out decades ago loves her.

But should that not happen, promise me this. Love Chloe, as I do.

She deserves your love, much more than I ever did.

With a sigh, I scrub my face, noting the postmark on the letter. Betsey sent it out the day before she passed, but the snow delayed delivery.

My friend made several cryptic comments before her procedure, but I assured her she would be fine.

Turns out I was wrong—on all counts.

Chloe isn't some spoilt city dweller. She's a woman who grew up without a mother. Had I known these facts beforehand, I would have had some stern words for Betsey. As it stands, I need to make it right with her daughter.

Scooting back my chair, I grab my coat and head for the door.

"A *genuine* apology, Dad," Natalie calls from the kitchen as I roll my eyes in her direction.

Got it, kiddo. Got it.

Chloe pulls open her front door, her face lined with apprehension. Way to make an impression, Aidan. "What can I do for you?"

Now that I'm not fuming at Chloe, I'm struck by her beauty and the fragility running just out of sight behind her calm facade. "I told the girls they can come by anytime, provided they ask you first."

Her brow furrows. Likely she thinks it's a trick. "Why the sudden change of heart?"

I hold out Natalie's letter. "I'm so sorry, Chloe."

"First time you've said my name. What is that?"

"A letter from Betsey. She wrote one for each of my girls."

"Emily mentioned something about a letter." Her slender fingers grasp the paper, but she makes no move to take it. "Figures she would write them and not me."

"Aren't you going to read it?"

"No. It's not for me." Pushing open the door, she motions me into the house. "Would you like some coffee?"

"I'd like to apologize. I didn't know the story, and I made

assumptions—*bad* assumptions—based on what information I had. I'd like to start over if we could."

"You don't want to hate me anymore?" That spark is so familiar. The same snarky sarcasm flowed from Betsey's lips.

"I'd like to see if maybe we could be friends."

"Is that what the letter told you to do?" Chloe inquires, barking out a laugh. "Thanks, but I'm good. I don't require your charity, Aidan."

Bullheaded, just like her mother. "Dammit, Chloe, it's not charity. I'm trying to admit I behaved like a horse's ass."

She plants her hands on her hips, shooting me a scalding glare. "You're trying or actually admitting to it?"

"You're a trying woman, you know that?"

"Likely a term of endearment, considering what you had thought of me."

With an aggravated scoff, I smack the wall. "Forget it. I'm sorry I wasted your time."

Chloe snakes out a hand, grabbing my arm. "Don't go. I'm… sorry I was so defensive. I feel like I've been under attack since I got here, and I'm tired."

"What have you eaten today?"

"Coffee."

"That's it?" It's past noon.

"Yeah. I forgot to eat."

"Unacceptable. Let's go. I'll buy you lunch, and you can tell me about the real Chloe."

She hesitates, but I'm not taking no for an answer. I'm a charming man when I want to be, and the woman has earned top-tier charm at this point. I grab her coat off the hook, holding it out to her.

"Come on, I'll get you some good old southern cooking. A favorite place of Betsey's."

Chloe takes the coat, and our fingers brush. For a moment, I forget to breathe. There's something about her. She stirs something in me. Even when I detested her, she still brought up a bevy of emotions.

Likely her connection to Betsey, nothing more.

I drive us to the local diner, and we settle into a booth. From my perch, I notice how the locals eyeball Chloe—some with an appreciation of her good looks, most with suspicion. I hope that when they see us together, they'll back off a bit.

I grab the menu, even though I know the thing by heart. "Besides me being a total ass, how is everyone else treating you?"

Chloe smirks, shaking her head. "Like a damn Yankee. You're a bloodthirsty lot when you don't like someone."

I bite back a grin. She's not wrong. "So much for southern hospitality, huh?"

"It's a myth." At least now she's smiling. Smiles suit her much better than scowls, especially when I'm the one who put the scowl on her face.

Tom, the local plumber, stops by the booth, extending his hand to Chloe. "I'm sorry about your Mama. She was a good lady. Welcome to the neighborhood."

Chloe's eyes widen in disbelief at the sudden one-eighty in the town's disposition, but she covers it well, shaking hands with Tom before he sidles to his usual table. "Are you the mayor or something?"

"Or something," I smile, stroking my beard. "I'm the local carpenter."

"It's *you*," she states, pointing a finger in my direction. "You're the one working on Betsey's house."

Nodding, I swig back some tea. "Guilty. I'd like to finish up, if possible. Unless you prefer hiring someone else."

Leaning back against the booth, she regards me with her dark eyes. "I don't know. Are you any good?"

Fuck, that got my dick's attention. "In many ways."

The only sign that my retort unhinges her is a slight widening of her pupils. Beyond that, she's cool as a cucumber. "So says you, at least."

"So says many people."

This time, the snicker escapes from her pouty smile as she turns her focus to the menu. "Are we still discussing carpentry?"

"Were we ever?" And just like that, I slide on my flirty cap, the charming bachelor who woos all the local women.

"I suppose you would be popular with the ladies who like that sort of thing."

No way I'm letting that comment slide. "What sort of thing?"

Glancing up from the menu, Chloe motions to my face, a smirk on her mouth. "The whole backwoods, lumberjack thing."

"Let me guess. Everyone wears suits and ties in New York, right?"

"No, we have lumberjacks, too. They've never held a damn ax, but they play the part."

Then she laughs, and it's by far the most beautiful sound I've ever heard. Her laugh puts Betsey's to shame, and that's saying something.

"You sound so much like your mom."

"You'll have to tell me about her one day."

"Gladly, but not today. Today, we're discussing you."

"I thought we were discussing lumberjacks," Chloe responds with a wink as a server strolls over to take our order.

Our server, Barbara, has long had the hots for me and judging by her cool countenance toward Chloe, she's none too fond of the fact that I have a dining partner. She takes Chloe's order, but the smile barely registers on her lips.

Until she looks my way.

"How about you, handsome?" Barbara's face brightens as she plants her hand on her hip, a saucy smile at the ready.

Barbara is beautiful, and I've danced around the idea of dating her, even though I doubt it would go much beyond a few fun encounters. But right now, I want to up the ante on flirting with Barbara for no other reason than to get a rise out of Chloe.

Why? No idea. Perhaps the fact that the gorgeous woman across the table from me seems immune to my appeal is the deciding factor.

I cross my arms and lean on the table, shooting Barbara a grin. "Barbara, do you like lumberjacks?"

Chloe snorts her coffee while Barbara narrows her gaze in confusion. "Beg your pardon?"

"Men like me. Beards, flannels."

"Absolutely. Who wouldn't?"

Swinging my gaze to Chloe, I shoot her a self-righteous stare. "See?"

"Any woman would be a fool to turn you down, Aidan Reid. I know I'm still waiting for my dinner invitation." With a last glare in Chloe's direction, Barbara heads to the kitchen, some extra hip shake thrown in for my viewing pleasure.

"Thanks, she's going to spit in my food now." Chloe releases a sigh, but I see she's trying hard not to laugh.

"No, she won't." Okay, I can't be positive about that fact. "I had to prove a point."

"Which is what?"

"Men like me are in high demand."

Chloe leans forward, close enough that I can see every freckle dusting her nose. "You had to stroke your own ego, is that it? Seems to me, if you were humbler, women would line up to stroke something else."

I sputter my tea, shocked by the words flying from her mouth. Her absolutely gorgeous mouth.

"Bet you never had a conversation like that with Betsey." Leaning back against the seat with a wink, she grins, biting her lower lip for effect.

Yep, Chloe Strickland is beyond tantalizing.

"You'd be surprised." Sitting forward, I motion toward her. "Start talking, Chloe. I want to know everything about you."

Thirty minutes later, I've learned three things about the beautiful woman sitting across from me: she's got a wicked wit and sense of humor, she's a successful writer, working for several high-end magazines, and I desperately want to screw her. Not a quick fuck either, but a long and leisurely exploration of her body. I bet money she's a screamer.

At least my money is on the fact I'll die trying to bring her to that level of excitement.

Unfortunately, sex isn't a possibility, and it has nothing to do with Chloe's less than enamored opinion of lumberjacks.

I have one rule when it comes to dating—the woman has to have kids.

Why?

Because I have kids. My family is complete and the last thing I need is to get wrapped up in a woman wanting more babies. I'm a single dad who dates single moms.

Pretty simple.

Chloe doesn't have children. I knew this before our breaking bread luncheon, although the knowledge is infinitely more painful now.

Still, rules are rules.

We finish our meal, complete with the requisite jokes and ribbing. By the end, I feel like we've known each other forever. I snatch the check before she gets a chance, earning a fake glower that doesn't reach her eyes.

On the short drive back, I point out some of the local haunts—the pub, post office, and grocery store. Pulling up to my house, I chew my lip as I glance at her snow-covered walks. "I'll blow out your driveway in just a bit."

"You don't have to do that. I'll be fine."

"I saw you earlier, Chloe. You're a bit unwieldy with the shovel, so I can sit back and laugh at you, or I can use the snowblower and be done in ten minutes. Your choice."

"When you put it like that," she mutters, a grin crossing her face. "Thanks for lunch, Aidan. Thanks for everything."

Shifting in the seat of my truck, I face her, my gaze inadvertently dropping to her lips. Hey, she has a sexy as hell mouth. I'm allowed to look, even if I can't taste. "Thank you for giving me a second chance."

"It better be worth it. *You'd* better be worth it," she teases, giving me a light jab in the arm.

She pops out of the truck, waving at my ex-wife who's standing in the yard. "Hi, Enid. How are you?"

"Just fine. Jeff and I left you a fruit basket. It's on your porch."

"You're so sweet. Thank you both."

"Is my ex-husband being nice to you?" Enid questions, quirking her brow at me.

"Tolerable." Chloe smiles at me, biting that full lower lip and once again sending my thoughts to the gutter. "Lucky for Aidan, he redeemed himself with some good old southern barbecue." With that, she disappears into her house, right after bending over in full view of me to grab Enid's gift.

Turns out, her peach is far more delectable than anything in that basket.

"Lucky for him, indeed," Enid mutters as I stroll toward her, shooting her an innocent look. "I see you two have kissed and made up."

"I don't know about the kissing part."

"You like her. I see it in your face."

"Doesn't matter. You know my rule."

Enid rolls her eyes, throwing up her hands in resignation. "You and your stupid rules. The girls said you want to keep them an extra day?"

"I want to take them ice skating. That cool with you?"

"Aren't we invited?"

"Sure, if you want to come, but I'm not buying you and Jeff hot cocoa."

"No, you're saving that sweetness for someone else," Enid retorts with a wink, pulling open her car door.

"I told you—"

"I call bullshit. I give it two weeks, tops." She's in her car before I have the chance to reply.

Typical Enid.

But she's wrong. No matter how beautiful Chloe Strickland is or how much I'd love to explore every inch of her curves with my tongue, she's off-limits.

End of story.

CHAPTER 4
CHLOE

Things are looking up.

First, I found an organic market in Asheville and blew way too much cash on all varieties of edible goodies. Let's be honest—wine and chocolate make everything better.

Second, I now know my way around Betsey's wood stove, so my ass is comfy and cozy.

Third... Aidan. He's not my usual type, yet there's something so endearing about him. He's witty, expressive, and good-looking in an offbeat, woodsman sense.

Okay, so the beard still irks me, but it's *his* face, right? Although, I do wonder what he looks like under all that fur. Maybe he needs the beard to cover a receding chin or weak jaw.

Or maybe he's so beautiful under that beard that I'd melt the second I saw him.

Much safer with the beard.

Mostly, bearded or not, it's nice to know I'll see a smile instead of a scowl with my next-door neighbor, or should I say, temporary neighbor. Once the work is completed on the house, she goes on the market, and I return to my regularly scheduled life.

But that is likely several weeks away, so I choose to focus on the beauty of the North Carolina mountains.

Wrapping a quilt around my shoulders, I step out onto the front porch, breathing in the crisp air.

"They make coats for this type of weather, you know."

Swinging my head to the right, I catch Aidan's teasing glance, his white smile cutting through his beard. "I prefer being a trendsetter, so I opted for a blanket. It's what us Yankees do, you know."

"Doesn't surprise me," he volleys back.

He really has a lovely smile.

"Chloe, what size shoe do you wear?" Natalie asks, a pair of ice skates slung over her shoulder.

"Six. Why?"

"Perfect. Emily has an extra pair of skates that will fit you."

Say what now?

"What am I doing?" I ask, taking a tentative step off the porch.

"Dad is taking us ice skating, and Mom and Jeff are meeting us at the rink. You have to come. It's tradition."

"Nat, she doesn't have to come," Aidan says, shooting me a smile. "Although you're welcome to join us."

"I've skated at Rockefeller Center."

"Perfect. Emily, grab your extra pair. Chloe, go get dressed." Just like that, a sixteen-year-old takes charge of the situation, hustling me into my house to change into proper attire.

Guess I have a new set of plans for the day. Here I thought I'd spend the hours looking at photos and binging Netflix.

Should I mention now that although I *have* skated before, I'm not very good? As in terrible?

Apparently, there is no time for that as Natalie tosses me a hat and hurries me to Aidan's idling truck.

Huh. Family time with someone else's family.

The ride to the rink is filled with the girls' chatter as they argue over the radio, but they all lose when Aidan flips to a classic rock station. His reasoning? My ride, my rules.

I love the way Aidan is with his girls. There is such genuine love and affection, with the requisite ribbing, of course. I remember that kind of camaraderie. My father was my best friend until the day he died.

We park next to Enid's car, and she pulls open my door, grasping my hands with a smile. "Chloe, you're a pleasant surprise."

"She can skate, Mom," Natalie interjects, jumping from the truck.

"Full disclosure. I haven't skated since I was fifteen."

"What happened to Rockefeller Center?" Aidan smirks, handing me a pair of skates. "Don't worry. We'll keep you upright."

Now it's Enid's turn to giggle, hiding a laugh behind her hand. "I highly doubt that's what you want, Aidan."

"There's a lady present," Aidan argues, doing his best to appear innocent.

"Where?" Enid and I inquire in unison, both dissolving into laughter.

Aidan rolls his eyes, but I see the levity in their green depths. "Never mind. My mistake. Let's go."

The girls rush ahead, with Enid and Jeff close behind, as they throw on their skates in a mad dash to hit the ice.

Me? I'm taking my time. Perhaps if I take *long* enough, I might avoid skating altogether.

"Are you stalling?" Aidan asks, sending a pointed glance toward my feet.

"Yes. I don't relish the idea of falling on my ass repeatedly, no matter how much padding I have back there."

His brows raise as he bites back a smile. "I'm leaving that one alone."

"Smart man." I focus on lacing up my skates, aware of Aidan's gaze on me. "You have your camera at the ready for the obligatory blackmail shots?"

"I'm waiting for you to stand up so I can judge for myself how much padding you have back there."

With a smirk, I push myself to standing, pivoting to give him a full view of my ass. In my defense, it's one of my greatest assets, and judging by the way his tongue flicks against his lip, his eyes glued to my rear, Aidan agrees. "Well?"

"I sure as hell don't want to leave it alone now." Aidan sighs, a grin splitting his face. "You have a great ass, and now, that's pretty much all I want to look at."

"I'm sure I can find something else to occupy your thoughts."

Our gazes hold, that all too familiar sexual energy crackling between us. We are the king and queen of flirtatious banter.

It seems my last comment upended Aidan as he struggles for a comeback. Instead, he aims for neutral conversation as he holds out his hand and inches me toward the ice. "Don't worry, I've got you, okay?"

I see the girls skating to their heart's content, making this whole sport look effortless. One glance at the frozen water, and I know I'm not going to look like them in any way. "Why don't you go ahead? Seriously. Have fun."

"I will have fun—with you. Come on."

With tentative steps, we set out on the ice, and within a few minutes, I'm only grasping him for dear life every other turn. He's a champ, never leaving my side, even though I can tell by his grace on skates he'd far rather be with his girls than bumbling about with me. Still, he provides words of encouragement, never once making me feel like a klutzy oaf. No worries, I feel that way *all* on my own.

After twenty minutes, I bail out, giving him some time to show off his skills.

I have a different aim. Hot cocoa and non-skid surfaces.

Settling onto a seat, I take in Aidan's effortless moves around the rink, his daughter Emily by his side. Those two have quite a bond. They remind me so much of my father and me when I was Emily's age.

"He likes you." Enid plops down next to me, a smile coloring her face.

"It's a step up from loathing me."

"He's a good man. An amazing father. Really kind heart, and he's damn good-looking if you like that type."

"Are you playing matchmaker?"

"Maybe. I think you two would be good together, despite his rule." Enid makes air quotes, rolling her eyes.

"Rule?"

"He only dates women with children."

"Ah, I see."

"But his rule is bullshit, and I'm pretty sure he'll figure it out. Especially now since you're here."

The chat is destined to go no further, as Aidan, Jeff, and the girls barge into our moment, their noses red and breaths frosting in the air.

Enid grabs Jeff's scarf, pulling him in for a kiss. Talk about love. Those two look like a couple of high school kids. "Come on, girls, Jeff and I will take you for hot cocoa. Aidan, you'll get Chloe home?"

"I got her here, didn't I? Didn't plan to make her walk back."

"What a gentleman," Enid jokes, pinching Aidan's cheek. "See you soon, Chloe. Call me if you need anything or if you want to chat."

Just like that, I'm alone again with Aidan.

A man who will *not* date me because I don't have children.

I'm going to ignore how that fact is bothering the hell out of me.

Why *wouldn't* he want to date me? I'm pretty, successful, disease-free, and reasonably sane, as sanity goes. But I'm a pariah, simply because I don't have kids?

I scoff under my breath. His loss.

He's not my type, anyway.

When we pull into Aidan's driveway, a few flakes are drifting to the ground. Have to hand it to Asheville; they love snow. "Thanks for today."

"Did you have fun?"

"I did. Thanks for keeping me upright." I hesitate, my hand on the door handle. "I bought this great bottle of wine and some cheese and crackers the other night. Would you like to join me for a drink?"

Aidan taps the steering wheel, considering my request. "Umm…"

"Please don't feel obligated. You don't have to."

"No, I'd like to." Now he swings that emerald gaze my way, and a flutter rushes through my body. "Funny, I was trying to figure out a way to keep the day from ending, but you did it for me."

With a mock sigh, I roll my eyes, a giggle escaping my lips. "Leave it to the woman to do everything."

Aidan snorts, turning off the truck. "No wonder you and Enid get along."

"We both have good taste."

I didn't mean for the words to come out sounding like some sexual innuendo, and I feel the flush crawl up my cheeks.

Gah, I'm so uncool right now.

Rushing from Aidan's truck, I make a beeline for my front door. It isn't like the man doesn't know the way—he's more familiar with this old farmhouse than I am.

We pull off our boots, shaking the bits of snow from our coats before Aidan heads for the stove, tossing on another log.

Me? I'm heading for the wine cabinet, pulling out a bottle of shiraz that I paid way too much for at the local market.

Even so, I feel the need to celebrate the little victories, and a friendship with Aidan is just the ticket.

"Will you open this for me?"

"Sure." Aidan takes the bottle, popping the cork with ease. "Viola, madam."

"Perfect."

We settle onto the enclosed porch, a tray of cheese and crackers in front of us, the fire from the stove warming every crevice in the house.

Aidan motions to the tools and lumber littering the back half of the house. "I'm sorry for the mess. I hoped to get it all done before the snow arrived, but nature had other ideas."

I scan the back room, still uncertain *what* it was Aidan hoped to finish. "What was my mother planning back here?"

Aidan's eyes twinkle as he snorts out a laugh. "Betsey wanted a conversation pit, sunken down two or three steps. According to her, she was bringing back the seventies."

My eyes widen, horrified. "But why?"

"I asked the same question. Several times, in fact. If you don't like that idea, I can do something else. Trust me, I argued Betsey on this point."

I chuckle, taking another swallow of the sweet red wine. "I'm glad it's not just me, but that sounds like a terrible idea."

"Agreed."

I chew my lower lip, aware of Aidan's emerald gaze on my face.

Friend zone, Chloe. Remember, you and Aidan will only ever be friends.

"I'd really love to create something cozy, with a fireplace. Like a—"

"Reading nook," we both say in stereo, our gazes holding.

"Exactly."

Aidan clinks my glass with his own. "I thought the same thing. Let's ditch her conversation pit idea—"

"Also known as a liability pit when someone drops into it headfirst. Likely me, as evidenced by my lack of grace on skates."

"Let's not do that. You have far too pretty a head." Aidan averts his gaze, but I notice the slight flush. At least I'm not the only one affected. "A small corner fireplace. Ambiance more than heat. Floor-to-ceiling bookshelves and a couple of overstuffed armchairs. A decorative window that will capture the morning light. Maybe stained glass."

I can't hold back the smile crossing my face. "That would be perfect. It's like you're in my head."

I try not to blush—again—when he smiles at me. Even through the thick beard, I can see his faint dimples. The truth is that the beard is bothering me less and less. Or maybe it's that I like Aidan more and more.

We chat about the revised house plans for the next few minutes, letting the warmth from the stove, the wine, and the conversation settle into our bones. Funny, the camaraderie we now share when only a couple of days ago we were mortal enemies.

"Can I ask you something, Chloe?"

"Sure."

"What happened with you and Betsey? I'd like to know the full story since my friend never saw fit to let me in on all her secrets."

Shifting on the couch, I tuck my legs under me as I chew the inside of my cheek, trying to formulate a response.

What happened? Good question. What, indeed?

"Betsey left New York when I was twelve. According to my dad, she wanted her freedom, and he wouldn't hold her fast, tethered to a marriage and child that didn't suit. It was radio silence for almost two years. Then one day, out of the blue, she calls me, wanting to pick up where we left off years earlier. I told her then where she could shove her maternal instincts."

"Understandable. You were at a very impressionable age. I know how crazy it's been with Natalie—all the emotional and physical changes happening. I try to be there for her, but she needs a female touch. It must have been hard on your dad, trying to cover both roles." Aidan moves next to me on the couch, his body a warm beacon in an uncertain world.

"He did the best he could. My father was a truly incredible man, and he adored me. I never once doubted his devotion. But he got sick with cancer when I was sixteen and died right before my eighteenth birthday. He made me promise him on his deathbed that I would reconcile with Betsey. When I was twenty-two, I caved to my father's request and came down here to visit. This was before she settled in Asheville. Betsey and I hadn't seen each other in a decade, and she implored me to move here, but I felt no kinship to the woman who shared my bloodline. I was still too angry. It took me another decade to get past the anger.

Still, during the last several years, we moved, ever so cautiously, toward a normal relationship. But life was busy for us both, and this Thanksgiving was to be the start of our new normal. I never planned on burying her during my visit."

Somehow, I manage the entire diatribe, but by the end, the tears are backing up in my eyes.

"I'm sorry, sweets. You deserved better than what life offered you." Aidan's hand settles on my leg, giving my knee a gentle squeeze. Without thinking, I bury my head against his chest, letting the tears have their due when his arms wrap around me.

He's by far the most comfortable place I've ever felt, and we pass the next few minutes like that, his hand stroking my hair as he murmurs words of comfort.

I pull back, wiping my face as I bark out a laugh. "I'm sorry. Guess I really needed a hug."

He thumbs away a few tears, his eyes soft with sympathy. "Don't be sorry. I've been told I give good hugs."

"You do. Quite possibly the best hugger ever, if I'm honest." Taking another swallow of wine, I feel its warmth flood my body. "Enough of *my* tale of woe. What's yours?"

"My what?"

"Your story. Why are you single?"

He shifts, considering my question. "I haven't found the right person. Isn't that what I'm supposed to say?"

"Only if it's the truth. Some men are perfectly content being single, with the occasional romp thrown in. Enid told me you only date single mothers."

Now he looks *really* uncomfortable. Probably afraid I'm about to light into him, desperate to convince him otherwise. "Yeah. It's my one rule."

"Makes sense."

"Does it?" His head flies up, eyes questioning. "I figured you would scoff at such a rule."

"Not at all. I have a rule, too. I don't date men with young kids. Not anymore."

I expect Aidan to relax, knowing I'm not gunning for a spot in his rotation, but instead, he clears his throat as his foot taps ceaselessly on the floor. "But you like kids."

"Absolutely. I love them, but I got burned by a single father, and now, I only date men who don't have children or whose kids are already grown. To be honest, I don't date much."

"I don't, either. Maybe we're too picky?"

"I think it's good to be picky. The worst thing in this life is settling for less than what you want."

He strokes his beard, his gaze focused across the room, and I know he's trying to gauge the best response. "So, looks like we definitely aren't dating."

I shake my head with a smile. Is it forced? Somewhat, but what's a woman to do? Aidan and I have rules, and those rules keep us firmly in the friend zone. "Looks that way."

"Does that mean we're friends?"

I sputter my wine, shooting him a mock glare. "Don't look so pained at the concept, Aidan. It's been known to happen before, often with a great deal of success."

He waits until I've set down my glass to lob a throw pillow at me. "Friends. Okay, let's give it a shot."

CHAPTER 5
AIDAN

Do you know my rule? The one rule I have about the women I date? Every day I spend with Chloe, it's becoming harder and harder to abide.

I'm working at her house every day of the week, and since she also works from home, we're always in each other's way.

Not that either of us seems to mind.

We're friends, which may be the most terrible idea I've ever had, albeit our safest option. But that title hasn't prevented me from wanting to know everything about her, while our strictly platonic relationship keeps us both at ease.

At least, until she bends over in front of me, and it takes everything I have not to grab her and sink balls deep inside her heat. Chloe has the most incredible ass I've ever seen, and I've never actually *seen* it.

Her tits are amazing, too, along with her face, and… her entire package is off the charts appealing. Throw in her kick-ass sense of humor, wit, and kind heart, and she's the most attractive woman I've ever known.

Betsey was right. Chloe and I would make an excellent match if it weren't for our rules.

But we have those rules for a reason, and we also have too much respect for one another to ever push the boundaries.

Not that the thought hasn't crossed my mind many, *many* times.

My only complaint with my new friend and employer? The woman keeps the house about a thousand degrees, to where I'm stripped down to my t-shirt as sweat drips off my nose. "You're one of those women," I remark, shooting her a grin. "Never warm."

"Aren't most women like that?"

"Not all of them. You're a special breed."

"Oh, I'm special, alright."

Yes, you are, Chloe.

She plops down on the floor near my work area, tossing me a bottle of water. "This looks amazing. You're very talented."

"In more way than one."

Chloe snorts her water, raising her bottle in a mock toast. "I'm sure you are, but for obvious reasons, we'll never know." She pauses, leaning back on her hands. "I'm sure there are a lot of women who would love to date you. I know that waitress in the diner was giving you the eye."

"Barbara? She's pretty obvious about her intentions."

"Does she comply with your rule?"

I nod, although I hate that word more every time I hear it. "She has a couple of kids."

"Perfect." Chloe's eyes narrow in my direction, but I notice the smirk on her lips.

Is it, though? I'm not so sure anymore—about anything.

What I fail to mention is Barbara, although a beautiful woman, stirs nothing in me.

Chloe, on the other hand? Let's just say I've jerked off several times to mental images of her naked and riding my cock.

"How many women are after you in this town?"

"Not many," I retort, finishing my water.

She chuckles, shaking her head. "Are you telling me you don't see the way women look at you?"

"Do you?"

"Do *I* look, or do I see other women looking?" Now she's testing me, that flirtatious gleam in her dark eyes.

"I know you don't like lumberjacks, so I'm pretty certain you're not looking. What other women are you referring to?"

Chloe pops to her feet, moving closer. "A few were trailing you down the aisles of the hardware store, drooling the whole way."

Now it's my turn to smile. While I won't admit it, for fear of sounding like an egotistical ass, I recall a busty blonde hovering in my vicinity during our recent jaunt to the store. "Nice thought, but I doubt that highly."

"Why do you doubt it?"

"What's so special about me?" Yes, I'm curious to know how Chloe sees me since I noticed she never mentioned if *she* is one of the women glancing my way.

"You're a good man. You adore your girls, which means you'd likely treat a woman with the same respect and affection. Hell, you even have a great relationship with your ex-wife. That is rare."

"Hmm."

"Like unicorn farting rainbows rare."

I bark out a laugh, shooting her a narrowed gaze. "That's likely the strangest compliment I've ever received. Wait, was that even a compliment?"

"Yes, Aidan. Keep up."

Resting the drill on the sawhorse, I cross my arms, eager to stay on this subject. "I like this conversation. Tell me some more good things about me."

"Ha. No."

"You brought it up. It's only fair."

"What a crock of shit. You just want me to stroke your ego," Chloe replies as she strolls into the adjacent room.

I'd really like you to stroke something else.

I lean back, catching her dark gaze. "Maybe, but tell me, anyway. I deserve a few accolades after saving you from a conversation liability pit."

Chloe tosses back her head, that tinkling sound escaping her mouth. God, I love her laugh. "Fine, but I'm not repeating this information, so listen up."

She clears her throat, and I prepare for yet another pithy comment. It's par for the course where Chloe is concerned. "Not only are you nice and talented, but you're also very good-looking. Don't think I haven't noticed what's hiding under that shirt. What woman doesn't love a hot body, covered in a thin sheen of sweat, playing with power tools?"

Well, that got my attention, along with the blush crawling up Chloe's cheeks.

"You think I have a hot body?"

"Without a doubt." With a cheeky wink, she disappears down the hallway as I take several breaths to center myself, running through every reason I need to stick with my current rule.

Only issue?

My rulebook never planned on Chloe.

Chloe makes me lunch every day, but it isn't something basic like a ham sandwich on a paper plate. She insists on putting out a spread, and she has proven to be a gourmet in the kitchen. I cook because it's a necessity, but it was never my strong suit. Just ask my girls their opinion of my cooking—they'll tell you all about it.

"That was delicious, thank you." I lean back in the chair, studying Chloe's face—the high cheekbones, wide eyes framed by dark lashes, full mouth, and smooth skin—and can't fathom how she's still single. "Why don't you have kids? I think you'd be an excellent mother."

I didn't mean to be that forthright, but it's the truth. Many women lack a true maternal instinct, but Chloe isn't one of them. She's terrific with my girls, and I know they adore her.

She's also sexy as fuck and smart as a whip. Basically, every man's dream.

It makes zero sense why she's still on the market.

"I always wanted kids. I was scared for a long time, terrified I would do what Betsey did to me. That it was somehow innate in my DNA. Then I met Charlie. He had two boys—two and three. Their mother had left them in much the same way Betsey left me, so I stepped into the mom role."

Impressive. My opinion of her bumped up a few notches, and trust me, it was already high. "That's not an easy thing to do, especially not when they're so young."

"I didn't mind. After Betsy deserted me, I suffered from a deep sense of inadequacy. Didn't believe I should put my needs first. Didn't feel I deserved to be first since I wasn't with my own mother, right? Anyway, I broached the topic of having another child, but Charlie had no interest in it."

Every word hurts my heart, especially the subpar treatment

from the man who was supposed to love her. "Damn. He wouldn't even consider it?"

Chloe shakes her head, a sad smile on her mouth. "He claimed he had his family already. So, I relegated myself to being their stepmom, and it worked until his ex-wife came back, and Charlie reconciled with her."

"Holy shit. How long had she been gone?"

"Six years. The kids barely knew her when she came back. She was a picture in a frame. A ghost. But Charlie wanted them to be a family again. A *real* family, per his words. I begged him to let me stay in touch with the boys, but he claimed it would confuse them. I wrote them each a letter, telling them I loved them, but I haven't heard anything since."

If I ever see Charlie, I'm punching the piece of shit in the throat. "I'm so sorry, sweets. That is awful on every level."

"By then, I was thirty-three, and most men were divorced with kids or married with kids or playing the godforsaken field and trying to recapture their youth. The next few guys I dated either had kids and didn't want any more or didn't want any to begin with. So, I decided to have a child myself."

Her last sentence jerks me upright. "You're having a baby?"

Chloe nods, intent on clearing the dishes. "That's the plan."

"When?"

"I was seeing a doctor in New York. He was going to inseminate me in January, but then this whole situation happened and threw me a bit of a curveball."

I click my tongue against my teeth, unsure what to say in response. Why does Chloe's plan to have a baby on her own feel so wrong to me? She's successful and financially independent, with a huge heart and love to share. Plus, tons of women raise children on their own every day, with no issue.

Still, it doesn't sit right with me.

Not one bit.

Chloe must pick up on my unease, cocking her head at me. "I take it you don't approve of my decision?"

With a shake of my head, I return to the moment. "It isn't that. You surprised me, that's all. It's not easy being a single parent, Chloe."

"I know, but it's not easy being alone, either."

"I know." Our gazes hold, and somehow, we intrinsically get one another. Our situations are different, but deep down, we're both lonely.

It's the first time I've admitted that fact, even to myself. I stay busy with work, the girls, my friends, and the occasional date, but in the early morning hours, I wake up alone.

The idea never bothered me before, but somehow Chloe's brutal honesty forces me to reflect on the state of my own life. It's not nearly what I hoped it would be. Despite what many might think, I long for that deep-seated love and companionship, too.

But I won't settle for just any woman. I want something magical, and magic is pretty damn hard to come by.

I see Enid's car pull into the driveway and glance at my watch. What's up with the early drop-off?

"Why don't you call it a day?" Chloe offers, joining me at the window. "Go spend time with the girls. You haven't seen them in a couple of days."

She's right, I miss them terribly when they're not at home, but I also don't want to leave Chloe, particularly not after she dissected her life for me, showing me all the skeletons hiding in her closet.

Every day it gets harder to leave her side. The knowledge that she's so close and yet so far away is driving me mad.

"I have an idea. I made barbecue."

Her brow furrows. "I thought you couldn't cook."

"Most things, but I make a mean barbecue. It's been smoking for two days out back."

"That's what I've been smelling. Well done, you, another bullet point for your list of positive attributes."

"Have dinner with us. The girls would be thrilled, and then we can all watch a movie afterward and pass out on the couch."

The smile on her face falters. "I'd love to, but I have a date tonight."

Her reply hits like a fist as I struggle to maintain a neutral countenance. "Already?"

Chloe laughs, waving her hand. "Yeah. This guy asked me out in the grocery store, of all places. Cornered me by the cantaloupes."

"What's his name? I might know him."

"Zeke Williams."

"Huh." That's the only response I can manage for the next few moments as I marinate on the fact that Chloe is going on a date tonight.

I hate it. Hate *everything* about the fact that Chloe is going out with Zeke Williams.

"Do you know him?"

I nod, forcing a smile, although it feels like my face will crack. "I do. Can't say we're friends, but we know each other. Be careful, okay? Call me if you need anything."

"I will. Thank you for listening. Tell the girls hello, and you'd better save me a plate of barbecue."

"No guarantee since you're too busy tonight."

She delivers a soft punch in my arm before retreating upstairs, no doubt to get gussied up for a date with another man.

I clean up my mess and leave Chloe's house five minutes

later, a deep sigh flowing past my lips as I contemplate marching straight to her bedroom and demand she cancels her date and spends time with me.

Do I know Zeke? I know him, alright.

Zeke is a tool, although the women of this town swarm around him like ants at a picnic. An egotistical oaf who resembles a male model. Not a hint of a lumberjack to be found.

Tugging on my beard, I cross into my yard, meeting Enid's knowing smile. "Why don't you invite Chloe over for dinner?"

"She has a date." The words fly from my mouth, clipped and short.

"Which you don't like at all."

"Not my business."

"Doesn't matter. You still don't like it. You know, you should show Chloe what a catch you are. You're actually ridiculously handsome when you're not channeling ZZ Top." Enid flicks the end of my beard, her lips pursed in disgust.

"Women love beards." I know this for a fact. Women are crazy about beards, right?

"Does Chloe love it, though?" She smirks because we both know that answer. "You're a gorgeous guy. Show it off. This fur on your face does *nothing* for you."

"What does it matter if I have a beard or not? She doesn't date men with young kids, and I don't date women without kids. You know my rule."

"Your rule is ridiculous."

"But her rule is okay?"

"Chloe got badly burned. That's the only reason she avoids dating men with young children. She doesn't want to endure that heartache again."

I'm reading too much into this, giving this idea way more life than I should. Still, the fact that Chloe is keeping her distance simply to protect her heart does something to me. It might sound crazy, but it gives me hope.

"Are you staying for dinner?" Time to regain the upper hand in this conversation.

Enid shakes her head, giving my beard one last flick. "No. Shave the beard. See what happens."

CHLOE IS MISSING OUT.

The barbecue is delicious, and my girls are full of amusing stories about their lives.

No way is her date nearly this much fun, especially not with Zeke Williams.

Still, I can't keep my mind from floating to my petite next-door neighbor, wondering how her evening is turning out.

Fucking Zeke.

"How's Chloe?" Natalie asks, shoveling more pork into her mouth.

"On a date with Zeke Williams."

My daughter's eyes light up. "He's handsome."

"What's so great about him?" Yes, I'm defensive. Every woman should realize what a tool the man is, not how good-looking he appears.

"He's gorgeous, Dad. For an old guy, anyway."

I scoff at my daughter's response. "Thanks, Natalie. The man is actually three years younger than me. I must be ancient."

"You look way older with the beard."

Another one harping on the beard. Tossing down my napkin, I glance around the table. "You girls don't like the beard?"

Six eyes focus on me, their heads shaking in tandem.

Here I thought it upped my cool factor, giving me a rocker edge.

"None of you like it?" Even Emily, who *always* has my back, scrunches her face in disgust.

"Sorry, Dad. You looked better before." Natalie drops a kiss on my head before dashing out of the room, her phone buzzing in her hand.

Later that night, after the girls are asleep, I stand in my bathroom, arguing with my reflection as I grab the clippers from the shelf. "This is *not* to impress Chloe. It's for the girls, who apparently despise the beard. Remember, this has nothing to do with Chloe or what she wants."

My reflection doesn't buy my bullshit excuse, either.

A final sigh echoes through the room as the clippers jump to life in my hand.

Here goes nothing.

CHAPTER 6
CHLOE

I peel open my eyes, scrunching them shut against the buzz saw screeching in my brain.

Unfortunately, the headache isn't from imbibing too much alcohol or partaking in too much fun with Zeke last night.

Nope, the pain is *because* of Zeke.

The man is an outstanding human specimen—just ask him—and he'll spend hours regaling you with tales of all his attributes. He only pauses long enough to convince you to spend the night with him.

What a great time you'll have. How amazing he is. Yada, yada, yada.

But Zeke didn't get lucky last night. The brazen egocentric struck out and no doubt is nursing his ego this morning, convinced I must be mentally deficient for turning him down.

I despise dating. It's exhausting, wading through banal conversations about the weather and your life plan. By the time I hit thirty-five, I knew within fifteen minutes, if a date had a snowball's chance in hell of going anywhere.

With Zeke, it only took thirty seconds, but he prolonged the torture for hours.

I wish I had dinner with Aidan and the girls instead.

I won't admit it aloud, but I love being around Aidan. There's a comfort in his proximity, combined with the ever-growing desire to rip off his clothes.

Hey, I have eyes, and those eyes did *not* miss Aidan's broad shoulders and chest under that thin t-shirt.

Dad bod? Not on that dad.

But it's pointless to focus energy on Aidan. He's my friend, and per his rule, that's all we'll ever be.

Thus, ending that tale before it ever began.

Judging by the banging sounds emanating from downstairs, my new buddy is already hard at work.

When I glance at the clock, I groan. It's almost eight in the morning, and I'm usually up before dawn. Sliding on some sweats, I shove my glasses on my face and throw my hair atop my head in a messy bun.

It might not be pretty, but I need caffeine in my veins before I contemplate my outward appearance any further. Besides, who am I trying to impress?

Aidan doesn't look at me like that. I could probably walk around in a bikini, and he wouldn't look twice.

Okay, he probably would. He *is* a guy.

A smile crosses my face as I enter the kitchen and the fragrance of coffee wafts up my nostrils.

Good man, Aidan.

I pour a cup before heading to the back of the house, eager to begin my daily banter with my resident hot carpenter.

"Good morning, Aidan. Want some more coff—" The question dies in my throat when Aidan looks up, a smile crossing his face.

His gorgeous, cleanly shaven face.

I know I'm gaping, but I can't stop staring at him. He was attractive before, but holy hell, it's suddenly three million degrees in here.

"You okay, Chloe?"

With an audible swallow, I nod, motioning to his face. "Wow. You shaved."

Aidan grins, running a hand across his chiseled jaw. Hiding a jaw that beautiful ought to be illegal. "I decided I had enough of the lumberjack look for a while."

"Wow." Perfect, now I sound like a daft idiot, repeating myself again and again.

Judging by the sexy smirk decorating his face, he loves every second of my reaction. "You approve?"

"Mm-hmm." Turning on my heel, I dart into the kitchen. I need to regain my equilibrium because Aidan has knocked any semblance of balance all to hell.

Loud footsteps fall in the hallway as he trails me to the kitchen, leaning against the doorjamb. "I can't tell if you like it or not."

"I like it." My voice, usually low and smooth, comes out as a high-pitched squeak, complete with full facial flushing.

Oh, the mortification.

Those dimples deepen as a grin splits his face. "What was that?"

Breathe, Chloe.

Finally finding my voice, I release a sigh as I brace myself against the counter. "I said I like it. You're just a bit disconcerting right now."

"Why is that?"

"Here's your coffee," I offer, thrusting a mug in his direction. "Just the way you like it."

But Aidan makes no move to take the mug as he crosses his arms over his muscled chest. I notice he's also wearing another thin t-shirt, only upping the sexiness factor. "Chloe, fess up."

What's the use in denying it? The man can tell by my idiotic blathering that he looks amazing. "Fine. I knew you were good-looking. I didn't realize you were *that* good-looking."

"You think I'm good-looking?"

"Yes, but I always thought you were good-looking." Can we please leave this conversation? Let's discuss a plague or something.

"On a scale of one to ten."

"I'm not answering that, you egomaniac," I laugh, feeling yet another flush climb my cheeks.

"Higher than seven?"

"Do you want more sugar in your coffee?"

"I want an answer."

"You look like a model, okay? Happy now?"

"Does that mean higher than a seven?" Even when he's intent on embarrassing the hell out of me, I can honestly say the man has the nicest smile I've ever seen.

Along with the nicest face.

I'm so screwed, or not, as the case may be.

With a groan, I grab my laptop and flip it open, even more aware of how ridiculous I appear next to his rugged good looks.

"I like the glasses."

Catching his gaze, my eyes widen. That was an unexpected segue. "I'm sure you don't. I look like a total nerd in them."

"Just the right amount of nerd. You should wear them more often."

"They're more comfortable, but most people prefer me without. You're the minority."

"I don't care what I am. I know what I like." That intense green gaze roams over my body, and I can feel the heat from across the room. "Besides, I always was a sucker for a sexy librarian."

"You think I'm sexy?" Hey, two can play this game. It's my turn now.

Aidan clears his throat, a slight flush coloring his cheeks. "You're a beautiful woman, Chloe. You already know that."

"Not what I asked." I'm not sure what it is about the way he's looking at me—words spoken without uttering a syllable—that keeps me pushing this conversation forward.

Aidan releases a nervous chuckle, averting his gaze. "How was your date with… Zeke?" I can tell by the way he spits out the man's name; he's as big a fan as I am.

"Long and torturous."

His gaze swings back to mine, those dimples on full display. "I'm sorry to hear that."

No, you're not, Aidan, and I'm ever so glad to see that relief crossing his face.

"He's a *true* egomaniac," I add, my nails tapping the wood table, my gaze never faltering from Aidan's face.

"He's a complete tool. The man doesn't deserve a woman like you."

"What do I deserve?"

"Everything."

That one word, barely audible as a throaty whisper, turns me on my head.

The air is positively thick, with the energy sparking between the two of us, an energy that's been growing exponentially every day.

Soon, we won't be able to hold ourselves back.

Soon, we won't want to anymore.

Aidan stands, moving toward the counter. "You know, your date with Zeke made me realize something."

"It did?" My heart pounds in my chest, hoping he'll announce how he's retiring his rule and what a dumb idea it was, to begin with.

Then, I'm ripping his clothes off.

"I decided I shouldn't sit home alone every night. I'm tired of being lonely, and our chat yesterday solidified that emotion. So, I took Barbara up on her offer. We're having dinner tonight."

And just like that, the air whooshes from my lungs as reality screeches into sharp focus.

All our flirtatious banter is just that—banter.

He had no intention of retiring his rules. No, he found a woman who played by them, instead.

I'm certain Barbara will be a better date than old Zeke, complete with a totally different outcome at the end of the evening. Once she sinks her hooks into Aidan, she won't let him go. Who can blame her?

I swig back a mouthful of coffee, letting the disappointment settle over me. As much as I'd like to rail against the idea, I can't be mad.

First, I have no right. I went on a date last night.

Second, Aidan deserves to be happy, and Barbara checks those boxes for him.

Me? I'm the saucy, pretty neighbor he enjoys flirting with, but it's nothing more than that. A friendship to pass the time while I'm in town.

"I hope you have a good time."

"Where did you two go for your date?" Aidan inquires, leaning on the counter.

"The pub."

He scoffs at my answer. "Zeke took you to a bar for your date?"

Guess I shouldn't mention how I also picked up the tab when he conveniently forgot his wallet. "It was fine. The food was okay. Where are you taking Barbara?"

"The steakhouse. The new one that just opened. Totally trendy and over the top, but that's what you do, right?"

Not with me, apparently.

Now I'm on the verge of tears—wonderful. I must be PMSing. That's my story, and I'm sticking to it. "She's a very lucky lady." Grabbing my laptop, I hug it to my chest. "I have a deadline for my articles, so I'm going to squirrel myself away upstairs. Thanks for making the coffee."

"No problem. I know where to find you if I need you."

I don't leave my bedroom for the next few hours. Instead, I sit perched on the bed, staring at a blinking cursor.

Thankfully, my articles are written since my brain can't focus on anything but the fact that Aidan has slipped through my fingers.

Not that we ever stood a chance, anyway. He doesn't date women like me. Childless women. I wonder if it would make a difference if I went ahead with the insemination and had a baby. Would I then be part of the club, eligible for his affections? Not forcing him to break his rule?

A wave of loneliness washes over me as I grasp a picture of Betsey, my tears falling onto the glass. "I wish you'd been around. I could have used a mom. It got lonely, wondering why I wasn't good enough. For anyone, it seems."

"Chloe, you got a second?" Aidan pushes open the door, his eyes widening at my tear-stained face. "Oh, sweets, are you okay? Why didn't you come to get me?"

"I don't like crying in front of people," I manage, wiping my eyes and leaky nose. Great, this day keeps getting better and better.

"It's actually healthy to cry, not keep it bottled up."

"I know, but I prefer to be an emotional mess on the inside. Smear lass mascara that way."

Aidan settles next to me on the bed, wrapping an arm around my shoulder. "I had you pegged all wrong. I thought you had abandoned your mother for some fancy life in New York City."

"I got that from the warm welcome you offered when I arrived." Despite the sadness, I chuckle. Something about Aidan's presence brings me peace of mind. "What did you need me for?"

"It's not important. It will keep." Aidan reaches forward, plucking a lash off my cheek. "Make a wish."

"I haven't done that in years."

"I do it with my girls, and I have it on good authority that you're never too old to stop making wishes. If anyone deserves a wish to come true, it's you, sweets."

Our gazes meet as a tremulous smile breaks across my face, and with a gentle blow, I send the lash floating off to new adventures.

"What did you wish for?" His gaze is damn near paralyzing, his hand pressed firmly against my back.

The truth? I wished for him, even though I know no eyelash anywhere can garner that wish true. I want to lie and come up with some glib answer, but his intense stare won't allow me that luxury.

"Chloe, what did you wish for?" His hand slides along my jaw, his gaze dropping to my mouth as my eyelids drift closed.

I feel his breath against my skin, beckoning of promises. Promises I've only dared dream about.

His lips drift against mine, his hand wrapping around my nape as I lean into the moment. Searching. Longing.

"Dad, where are you?"

We break apart—before we even started—with the realization of what *almost* happened, crossing Aidan's face and, I'm sure, matching my own shocked expression.

We almost kissed. If his daughter had been ten seconds later, we would have kissed. If left to our own devices, we might never have stopped.

"What's up, Natalie?" Aidan calls out.

"Are you upstairs?" Lovely, now it looks like we were having personal playtime.

"I'm talking to Chloe." Shaking his head, he glides his fingers along my arm, a rueful smile on his face. "I better go see what she needs."

Turns out Natalie needs her father to find a slip of paper for her class the next day, and it's buried somewhere in their house. After an hour, I realize he isn't coming back, which is probably for the best.

No, it's definitely for the best, no matter what my heart screams.

I grab my phone and send him a quick text.

Chloe: *I'm turning in early, but I wanted to wish you a good time tonight. I hope you and Barbara have fun.*

Do I mean what I write? Not at all, but this is what nice friends do, even if they're feeling overwhelming emotions for the man about to embark on a romantic evening with another woman.

I pour myself a glass of wine and prepare a charcuterie tray for one before plopping down on the couch for a night of reruns. But a quick glance out the window shows Mother Nature's artwork painting the sky in shades of red and orange, and I can't resist the urge to step outside for a closer look.

You don't get too many fantastic sunsets in Manhattan. The buildings block the view.

"I thought you were going to bed."

Turning my head, I offer Aidan a low whistle. The man cleans up well. His button-down shirt is practically bursting across his pecs with the sleeves rolled up to showcase his fantastic forearms, while his dress jeans accentuate his amazing ass... and package. Not that I'm looking—much. "Look at you. You look wonderful."

"I decided against a tie. Thought it was too much."

Giving him a thumbs up, I bite back the dread in the pit of my stomach. "Perfect as is. Are you headed out?"

"I am. Wanted to get Barbara some flowers. Do guys still do that? It's been a while."

Tears fill my eyes, but I blink them back. "See? I knew you'd treat a woman right. She'll love getting flowers. Perhaps a bouquet of lilies or something colorful." Great, now I'm giving him advice on wooing the woman who's desperate to jump him.

"You like flowers, Chloe?"

"Sure." What can I say? I can count on one hand the number of times I've gotten any? That four of those five bouquets came from my dad, and the other one I purchased for myself when the guy I was dating forgot my birthday?

Best to keep this conversation short and simple.

"Have fun. I'm headed to bed now, but I had to look at the sunset." I return my gaze to the sky, in awe of the beauty of this area. "She is so beautiful, without even trying."

"Yes, she is."

When I glance back at Aidan, he isn't partaking in the sunset. His gaze is focused on me, and I fight back an overwhelming urge to tell him to forget Barbara and spend the evening here. Sans clothing.

Instead, I shoot him a last smile and duck inside my house, sneaking a peek out my window to watch him drive away into another woman's arms.

CHAPTER 7
AIDAN

I skipped out on getting laid last night. Oh, Barbara was more than willing, and I'm sure the fancy restaurant and flowers only sweetened the deal. The woman even offered to suck me off in my truck, and although my dick threatened anarchy, I refused her advances.

It wouldn't have been right. Barbara was a bit tipsy, and I couldn't stop thinking about Chloe.

Couldn't stop thinking about how close I came to tasting her lips or the disappointment in her face when Natalie interrupted our moment.

I have to face facts. I want Chloe. Bad. But it's different now. I've wanted to strip her down and kiss every inch of her body since that first diner lunch, but somewhere along the way, my feelings have deepened.

Besides spending time with my girls, Chloe is the only thing I look forward to every day. I felt like I was cheating on her during my dinner with Barbara, which isn't fair to either woman.

So, I bought Barbara a top-of-the-line steak dinner, enjoyed some casual conversation and even a twirl around the dance floor at the local bar, and then dropped her safely at home.

It was the right thing to do, even if my dick and I aren't on speaking terms at the moment.

Staring at my reflection, I run a hand over my jaw. Barbara was more than disappointed about me changing up my look, which seems almost laughable, considering Chloe's reaction.

God, Chloe is adorable when she blushes, and I wonder what kind of thoughts she was thinking about me to bring on such a flush.

I'd be happy to show her firsthand.

If only it were that simple.

Why can't it be?

The thought hits me hard and fast, as if my reflection is challenging my rules, calling me out for being too stringent.

My reflection and I agree on one thing—this attraction to Chloe is reaching a breaking point. Something is going to give, and soon.

I stroll next door an hour later, letting myself in with the spare key Betsey gave me a few years back. Chloe doesn't seem to mind that I've kept it. Deep down, I think it makes her feel safe. "Morning."

"Hi, there." Chloe sits perched at the breakfast bar, clad in her usual leggings and sweatshirt. On any other woman, it's the antithesis of sexy. But not Chloe. The shirt is frayed at the collar, baring one shoulder that just begs to be kissed. Her upswept hair reveals the smooth expanse of her neck, and now I'm nursing another hard-on.

"You okay this morning?" I ask, shifting my pants and trying to think benign thoughts.

She smiles, but it doesn't reach her eyes. Instead, there's a tension in the air, no doubt from my date the night before. "Great. How are you?"

No way in hell are we going to waste time with blasé conversations. It's time to get it out on the table before I sweep everything *off* the table and take Chloe on top of it.

Not a bad idea, actually.

Grabbing a mug, I help myself to some coffee before leaning against the counter. "You sleep well?"

She shrugs, her eyes averted.

Yep, she's being distant. "Don't talk so much, Chloe."

"Sorry. I'm just going through some legal paperwork."

Walking behind her, I glance at the computer screen, leaning in closer than necessary. Am I pushing her buttons? I'm sure as hell trying. "Real estate agent? Are you selling?" That news hits like a fist, the idea that this petite, perky, sexy as fuck lady won't be next door for the duration.

"I'm weighing my options." Turning on the barstool, she ducks under my arm, putting more distance—physical and otherwise—between us. "You're in a good mood."

Actually, I'm about three seconds away from ripping her clothes off, but I opt to play with her a bit as I bite back a smile. "I guess I am. Do you know why?"

"I'm sure I could figure it out."

No, Chloe, your guess is all wrong.

"So, dating is weird, isn't it?"

"It can be."

"When do women normally…"

"Put out?" Her expression is downright pained now.

Do I keep treading? Damn right, I do. "Jeez, what a way to put it."

"I apologize for insulting your delicate tendencies. Knocking boots, a better term?"

"Not really."

"But that is what you meant?"

"Yes. Is it normally on the first night?"

The hint of a smile falls from her face. "Not with me. But it's different for everyone."

"You didn't sleep with old Zeke?"

"Definitely not," she grimaces, shaking her head.

"Hmm. So, the first night isn't usually—"

I watch the temper flare across her face. She does *not* want to discuss this topic any further. "I guess you got lucky, in more ways than one. What did she think of your new look?"

Running a hand over my jaw, I chuckle. "She prefers the beard."

"She's an idiot."

"I tend to agree with you." I opt to keep pushing. I'm treading a razor's edge, uncertain of where Chloe's head—and heart—lie. "She couldn't kiss worth a damn, either."

That did it. Chloe's head shoots up as her eyes narrow. It's only an instant, but I see it—jealousy. I've never felt so damn relieved to see that emotion in a woman. "I'm sorry to hear that."

"Are you?"

"Not especially. Likely a lousy lay, too."

"I didn't sleep with her."

"Really?" She's trying to remain casual, but I see her posture relax with my admission.

"Nah. Not my style."

"I like your style. It's refreshing to know there are men out there who aren't just looking for a quick lay."

"I'm not opposed to a quick lay, but I prefer to take my time. However, when you only have a few minutes, ripping off your clothes and bending you over the counter sounds like a fantastic idea." My gaze holds hers, daring her to look away. Daring her to deny what is building between the two of us. What's been building for the past month.

Now the flush is back, as she stands there, biting her lower lip and looking so damn good I'm having trouble containing myself.

She wants me. I want her.

"Admit it, Chloe."

"What?"

"Admit you hated the fact I went on a date as much as I hated you going on one with Zeke."

"It's not my business." But her face belies her words.

"Maybe you should make it your business."

"What about your rules?" She skews her mouth to the side, those wide-set eyes regarding me with feigned indifference. But I see the spark, and I know she's as tied up about this situation as I am.

"What about yours?"

The peal of her landline slices through the growing sexual tension like a hot knife through butter. Crossing my arms over my chest, I huff out a sigh, unsure how I feel about anyone daring to interrupt us. "Looks like you're saved by the bell. But Chloe?"

"Yes?"

"I really hope Zeke was a terrible kisser."

"I wouldn't know."

The god-awful ringing continues, but Chloe makes no move to take the call. Instead, she moves inches forward, every step bringing her closer to me. "Why would you hope it was a terrible kiss? Don't I deserve spine-tingling, orgasmic kisses?"

Finally, the ringing ceases, her final question dangling like the ripest fruit, demanding to be plucked.

A question I'm finally going to answer with brutal honesty. "Absolutely, all over your body, but not from him. Never from him."

As if in some technology-ridden nightmare, the damn phone peals out its ghoulish call again, determined to impede on our moment.

"They don't seem to be giving up. You'd better get that."

With a final bite to her lip, Chloe slips past me into the other room to answer the call, pivoting away from my heady stare. I've unhinged her, which is precisely my plan.

Time to drive my intentions home—in no uncertain terms.

Stepping to the edge of the room, I lean against the doorjamb, focusing my gaze on the ceiling. To the outsider, I appear at ease. My words, however, are anything by innocuous, flowing unbidden from my mouth. "Kisses covering every inch of your body, Chloe, but only from me. No one else."

At least I voiced my feelings, even if she didn't hear me.

With a last smirk in Chloe's direction, I return to my work area, intent on settling my feelings and ever-present erection.

"Well, that was interesting."

I sneak a glance up at Chloe as she leans across my sawhorse. "Was it? What did they say?"

"Not them. Me, trying to act normally after hearing you say you want to kiss every inch of me."

"You heard that?" There goes my heart, racing again, knowing it's all out in the open.

"The more important question is, did you mean it?"

"We both know the answer to that."

She nods, winding her way around the sawhorse and positioning herself directly in front of me. "What do we do about it?"

So many options, beautiful. Tons and tons of positions—I mean, options.

Moving flush against my body, she traces a line down the front of my shirt, my muscles flexing as her slender fingers drift over me. "Too bad I don't believe in casual sex. I bet we'd have an unforgettable time together. But I don't share, especially not a man like you. I'd keep you all to myself. But that's not how you plan to play it, is it Aidan?" She presses a finger to my mouth before I can answer. "You don't need to say anything. I already know the answer, which is why I will continue to dream about you every night and imagine that real life would be that much more incredible."

Rising on her tiptoes, she wraps her hand around my neck, pressing those soft lips against mine.

There's no pressure, no asking for more, just existing in this moment.

Together.

The only trouble? I want more. Much, much more. But before I can react, wrapping my arms around Chloe and proving I have no intention of sharing either, she pulls away, a soft smile coloring her mouth.

"In another life, I would make you fall madly in love with me."

Then, she turns and walks away, leaving me with a cock straining for release and my blood pounding in my ears.

What Chloe doesn't realize is I don't need another life. I'm falling madly in love with her in this one.

I'VE SPENT THE BETTER PART OF THE AFTERNOON running every scenario through my head, every reason why I shouldn't march upstairs and claim Chloe for myself.

The reasons—*my* reasons—that made sense a month ago

seem ridiculous now. But am I leading with my heart or my head?

See, I loved Enid. I still love Enid in a different fashion. But it was *never* this powerful, over-the-top, ridiculous attraction. That's why our marriage worked for so many years… it was more friendship with the occasional screw thrown in for kicks. When Enid met Jeff, she found her passion, and I'm thrilled for them both.

As for me, I've experienced plenty of passionate moments, but none I couldn't live without.

Until Chloe. I've never even touched her, and yet she's all I think about.

You only date single mothers, and Chloe wants a baby. In fact, she's planning on having a baby. Way too sticky a situation. Snap out of it, man.

Hell, maybe I should have slept with Barbara last night. Perhaps I should date her. She's attractive, smart, and personable—all excellent qualities—and if I wasn't a decent guy, I'd jump on that ship.

But dating Barbara would be unfair to us both. Her, because I'm in love with Chloe and me, for the same damn reason.

A loud crash sounds from upstairs, startling me from my reverie. Taking the steps two at a time, I find Chloe on the floor next to an overturned chair, a pained expression on her face as she clutches her ankle.

I kneel by her side, gently pressing the joint. "Are you okay? What happened?"

Chloe winces, pointing to a box perched on top of the bookshelf. "I slipped trying to get that box."

Leaning back on my haunches, I shoot her my best glare. "I'm right downstairs. Why didn't you ask me to get it?"

"I'm stubborn? Bull-headed? Pain in the ass? Take your pick," she mutters, struggling to stand.

With a chuckle, I scoop her petite frame into my arms, noting how right she feels pressed against me. "I'm going with a mix of all three, so you're lucky you're cute."

Chloe smiles, wrapping her hands around my neck. "I have my moments. Hopefully, I didn't do any permanent damage."

I have some medical training, so my guess is she twisted it. How seriously, I'm not sure. "I used to work as an EMT, so I'm fairly certain it's not broken. But I will wrap and ice it for you—downstairs, because that's where you're moving for the next few days."

Without waiting to hear her arguments, I carry her into the family room, depositing her on the sectional sofa. Thankfully, Betsey believed in comfort over looks since Chloe is now relegated to the couch.

Unless I take her home.

Do I want to? Absolutely, but I know where she'll end up—naked, in my bed, as I deliver my own brand of care.

But the problem lies in the fact that I can't give Chloe what she wants, so it's best to keep some distance, no matter what my heart says.

Her wide brown eyes regard me, a small smile on her mouth. "Is there anything you can't do? Build houses, check. First aid, check."

"I've been told I'm pretty damn good in other areas, too."

Now, why did I say that? Is it true? According to my past liaisons, it's more than true, but that's not the point. I just decided to put distance between Chloe and me. Still, every time I open my mouth in her vicinity, a flirtatious sentiment drops out.

Her smile widens. "I'm fairly certain that's a guarantee. Ouch," she yelps, grasping her ankle again.

"Stay there. I'm running to my house for supplies." I hurry home, grabbing the first-aid kit and ice pack. On the way out, I pull the tins of barbecue from the fridge. At least this way, I ensure Chloe eats tonight.

Settling next to her on the couch, I pull off her shoe and sock. Figures she has the prettiest feet I've ever seen, too. Smooth and soft, with brightly painted nails. Ticklish, too, judging by the way she jerked her foot when I grabbed it. Best not to do that again, at least not until she's healed. Then, it would be fun to torture her a bit.

I wrap her ankle, sliding the ice pack against the bandage. "There, I'll get you some pain pills."

"Can I have wine instead?"

Smiling, I nod. "Sure. I brought over the barbecue from the other night. Thought we could eat it for dinner."

"You're staying?"

It's hard to determine from her surprised look if she's happy about this concept. "I figured we could have dinner and watch some television. Maybe tease you as you try to hop around the house."

She chews her lower lip, her fingers plucking the blanket. "Aren't you seeing Barbara?"

"I wasn't planning on it, but I can leave if you'd prefer."

"I'd like you to stay."

I refuse to look a gift horse in the mouth. Returning to the kitchen, I heat up the food and pile everything onto a tray, complete with the requisite wine.

Chloe accepts the bowl with a smile, shifting to a seated position. "Thank you, Aidan. No one ever takes care of me."

Her words give me pause as I realize no one takes care of me, either. But somehow, it's sadder coming from Chloe. Such a beautiful woman should have a man doting on her, not taking her for granted. "This is nothing. Wait until you have the flu."

"Will you hush? Do *not* put that out there," she huffs, digging into the food. "This is delicious."

"Better than pub food?" Yes, I had to get that one in there, a reminder of the meal she missed while dining with Zeke.

"I didn't have to pay for this, either."

I toss down my plate, scowling at her. "Wait, just a damn minute. He made you pay?"

"He forgot his wallet." She shushes me, holding up her hand. "I know it's a bullshit excuse, but I wasn't about to walk out on the server."

"Chloe, if you go out with him again, I'm personally kicking your ass."

"Kicking or kissing?" she responds with a wink.

That's got my dick's attention, and she knows it, judging by her sultry smirk as I shift on the couch. "Definitely the former if you date that asshole again."

"And if I don't?"

I can't be sure if the wine is going to her head or if this is our new and improved sexed-up banter, but every cell in my body screams to grab her close. "Guess you'll have to wait and see."

Is it a cop-out? Absolutely, but my restraint is nonexistent where this woman is concerned. The last thing I need is her regretting us, should something happen.

Seeing that emotion on her face is more than I could handle.

"What a gyp," she laughs, downing some more wine. "Your loss because I have a great ass." She turns away, grabbing the television remote. "Ready for a marathon session?"

What I'm ready for is Chloe, but it seems we both know moving forward is a bad idea. It's sexy as hell to dance along that edge, but when we cross the line, we can't ever turn back.

So, we opt for the safety of our friendship, knowing how much we want each other but refusing to give in to the temptation.

We're being smart, and I'll keep telling myself that until I believe it.

I STIR AWAKE, MY EYES TAKING IN THE UNFAMILIAR surroundings. Okay, I'm not in my bed. Glancing down, I smile, tightening my arm around Chloe's sleeping form.

Seems that after a couple of movies, we fell asleep on the couch, and sometime during the night, we gravitated to each other's arms.

Stroking her dark hair from her face, I let my gaze wander over her. She's so beautiful, and even now, half-asleep, my heart races from her proximity.

I want to kiss her.

Deep and slow, taking my time to learn every inch of that beautiful mouth.

Leave her breathless and begging for more.

Begging for me.

"You are so comfortable." She snuggles closer, a soft groan flowing past her lips. "It's going to hurt if I move."

Pressing a kiss to her head, I nod. "Let me get you some aspirin and another ice pack." I slide out from under her, the chilly morning air seeping into my bones.

Tossing a log on the stove, I stumble into the kitchen to make coffee but pause when I notice the time.

Gripping the edge of the counter, I try to slow my breathing.

I don't sleep—three to four hours per night, maximum. Even

then, it's often fitful. But last night, with her body pressed against mine, I slept for seven straight hours.

That's never happened before.

"Why?" I hiss under my breath, feeling my control over the situation slipping away. "Of all the women in the world, the one I feel something for is the one woman I can't have."

CHAPTER 8
CHLOE

"I heard you're broken," a familiar voice calls down the hallway.

"Come on in, Enid," I yell from my perch on the couch.

Enid sits next to me on the couch, nodding toward my injured paw. "How are you feeling?"

"Like a total klutz? Actually, I'm much better. The first few days sucked, though. Thanks for my care package."

This woman is amazing, constantly dropping off goodies with a silly note attached. Enid is great at brightening my day. "No worries. Chocolate makes everything better."

"It must because I'm practically full weight-bearing now."

Enid sniffs the air. "What is that delicious smell?"

"Chicken chili. It's been cooking all day. Would you like to stay for dinner?"

"Are you sure there's enough?"

"There's a ton of food, more than enough for everyone. Can you invite the girls, too?"

She smiles, motioning toward the house next door. "What about Aidan? I'm sure he's hungry."

I fix my gaze on the blanket. "I'm not so sure about that. Barbara was over there earlier."

"Really? What's that about?"

My answer? A shrug, because honestly, I don't want to know. Despite his less than stellar review of their evening, I've seen her leave his house twice in the past week.

After our unintentional snuggle-fest on the couch, Aidan has put some breathing room between the two of us, even focusing on jobs outside of my mother's house.

It's for the best, really.

No point falling for someone I can't have, even though I've already fallen hard for him.

"Aidan is a good man, but you know that already."

"What happened with you two? I probably sound terribly forward for asking, but you get along so well. Most exes are not that friendly."

"We weren't either, for a while, but we wanted to ensure the divorce was as painless as possible for the girls. Divorce is hard enough without throwing in personal grievances that have nothing to do with the kids."

"I wish more people handled divorce like you and Aidan. After my mother left, she and my father only spoke once, and that was after his cancer diagnosis. She called to apologize, but my father had forgiven her long ago. It was *me* who held onto the grievances."

"I'm sorry that was your experience. Aidan's parents were terrible, which explains why he was so desperate to escape that house. We were high school sweethearts who rushed headlong into adulthood. We thought we could handle it, but we were wrong. Suddenly, we were in our late twenties with the distinct feeling that life had passed us by. Mia was a whoops. We hadn't had sex in two years, and then one night, we did, and bam, Mia was born nine months later."

"Wow. Fertile myrtle."

"No, it's all him," Enid remarks with a grin. "By the time she was born, we were barely speaking. I met Jeff in the grocery store six months later. Totally didn't see him coming."

"How did Aidan react?"

"I think it relieved him, knowing he wasn't the only one no longer in love."

"That explains the camaraderie."

"We made certain it wouldn't get ugly. We adore each other, just like a brother and sister... who happen to have three children."

"You have beautiful daughters." It's the truth. Their girls are gorgeous inside and out, much like their parents.

"Thank you. Don't you want any kids?"

I release a groan, looking skyward. "I do. In fact, I planned on having a child this coming year."

Unlike Aidan's expression of shock, Enid simply nods at my declaration. "You'll be a wonderful mom."

"I hope so. Anyway, it hasn't happened yet, so who knows if it will?"

"What if you fall in love between now and then?"

"With whom?"

Enid catches my gaze, and I know she sees through my blasé response regarding love. Her grin solidifies it. "Well, I know a certain someone who looks way better now than he did a couple of weeks ago."

"Yes, he does." The man is a whole new level of sexy, if I'm honest.

"He needs to find a good woman."

"There's Barbara. They went on a date the other night, and she's been around a few times this week. Unfortunately for him, she was a fan of the beard."

"He didn't shave the beard for his date with Barbara."

"I know, but I'm sure he wanted to make a good impression and instead shot himself in the foot. He's a handsome man. She's a fool if she doesn't see it."

"He shaved the beard for you. He knew you didn't like it." She pats my knee, sending me a knowing smile. "He likes you very much, Chloe."

"He's a wonderful friend."

"He's more than that."

"He isn't. We haven't—" I sit up, feeling the panic set in.

"Relax. I'd be thrilled if you two got together." She stands up, grabbing her purse. "Since you've been amazing enough to prepare dinner, I'll run out and grab dessert. See you back here in a couple of hours."

Good to her word, Enid walks back into the house precisely two hours later, her family in tow. The girls make a beeline for the family room, eager to look through Betsey's photo collection, while Jeff sets about tending the fire.

The only person missing is Aidan. I guess he had plans with Barbara again.

At least I didn't get too dressed up. I changed into a simple sweater dress and applied a hint of makeup, but nothing outlandish. Nothing that looks like I'm trying too hard to impress the man who isn't here.

Swallowing back the disappointment, I focus on prepping the chili fixings, smiling as laughter wafts in from the other room. I haven't had enough laughter in my life—not by a long shot.

"Hey, sorry I'm late," a voice says behind me.

Spinning around, I can't hold back the smile crossing my face.

Aidan is here, looking gorgeous in a flannel and jeans. Turns out I *do* like the lumberjack look, at least on him. "You came."

Aidan grins, holding out a bouquet. "I had to get these first."

I bury my nose in the purple roses, feeling the tears back up in my eyes. It's the first time a man, outside of my dad, has ever brought me flowers, and the emotions are swiftly becoming overwhelming. "They're lovely. Purple is my favorite color."

"I had a feeling. Glad I chose correctly."

"You didn't need to buy me flowers."

"You're cooking dinner for this crazy crew. Some flowers are the least I can do."

My glow fades at his words. The bouquet is still as lovely, but it's not a romantic gesture. Rather, a hostess gift. "Let me put them in some water."

"Thank you for doing this."

"It's my pleasure. It's nice not eating alone."

"I know the feeling. I'm alone all week, remember?"

Not lately, Aidan.

"I never thought of it like that. You always seem so busy."

Aidan leans on the counter, a sexy smirk playing on his mouth. Glad to see he's decided to stick with the clean-shaven look. No matter what Barbara says, the man is gorgeous without the damn beard. Okay, he's gorgeous either way.

I still prefer seeing his face.

"I've got an idea. We should have dinner together a couple of times during the week. We're right next door to each other, and that way, we aren't alone."

"That way, you don't have to cook," I retort with my usual sass.

"Also, a bonus. What do you say?"

But I don't answer him, rather shoot back my own request. "Can you open a bottle of wine?"

If my response bothers him, he doesn't let it show, instead focusing on the wine rack. "How about this one? Oh wait, this is expensive."

"Open it."

"You don't want to save it for a special occasion?"

"We're all together. That *is* a special occasion."

His dimples deepen with the smile crossing his face. "I like your logic."

He pops the cork as I continue the food prep, sad that it appears our flirty banter has been shelved in lieu of platonic camaraderie.

That idea should make me happy.

It doesn't.

Suddenly, Aidan is right next to me, and my heart jumps at his proximity. I suck at appearing disinterested.

Then he touches me, his fingers brushing against my neck as he pushes my hair over one shoulder. "You look beautiful, Chloe. Something indelibly sexy about the way that dress hugs your curves, giving me just a hint of what lies underneath. Whets my appetite."

Suddenly it's three thousand degrees in the kitchen as a full-body flush dances across my skin.

My mistake.

Seems the flirty banter is not only still in force but has also been kicked up a notch. The only problem? I know he's been spending time with Barbara, and likely the woman is warming his bed.

Determined to stay my course, I maintain a staring contest with the peppers, chopping them into bits.

"You're blushing."

"Am I? Must be the heat in the kitchen." Pivoting, I thrust a bowl into Aidan's hands. "Will you take this to the table?"

Aidan's sexy smirk widens as he leans in, pressing a soft kiss right underneath my ear and setting off a series of sparks in my body. "You're very flustered right now. I wonder why."

He sends me a wink before turning on his heel, leaving me at the counter, my heart pounding and hormones racing.

How in the world will I survive dinner?

Ten minutes later, I'm about to find out as the entire group crowds around Betsey's dining room table, the hum of laughter and conversation reverberating off the walls.

This is what family is about.

For the first time since my father died, I don't feel the pang of loneliness. Raising my glass, I toast the friends gathered.

After that, they waste no time digging into the food, except for Natalie, who has a far more pressing question. "Dad, why was Barbara at the house again?"

Aidan clears his throat, shrugging. "I don't know. She stopped by, claiming to need some repairs on her kitchen."

My guess? She stopped by for a quickie, but I choose to keep that tidbit to myself.

"Ugh. Why did you go on a date with that woman?" Enid pipes up, shaking her head.

"I'm sure she's not that bad, aside from being a lousy kisser," I mutter, sending Aidan a conspiratorial wink.

Enid's frown grows. "You kissed her? How is that even possible with those lips? I swear she has more Botox than a botulism lab. I do not approve, Aidan."

"Noted, Enid."

Enid stabs at her food, clearly agitated with his choice of dinner partner. "Are you going out with her again?"

The din quiets as Aidan glances at me. "I wasn't planning on it."

A surprising turn of events.

"How come?" I ask, trying to conceal the joy running rampant in my veins.

"She's a nice woman, but I'm not interested in her. Not like that."

"Which means," Enid interjects, "you're interested in someone else."

There goes my damn heart again. Off to the races. "Are you?"

Aidan focuses his eyes on his plate, wiping his hands on his napkin before meeting my questioning gaze. "Yeah, I am, but it's a complex situation. Still, she makes me feel..." he drifts off, averting his gaze.

I get it. This is one hell of a sticky subject.

"Can we talk about something other than my dating history?" Aidan inquires, earning a chuckle from Jeff.

"Fine," Natalie shrugs, turning her attention to me. "We can discuss Chloe's dating history. How was your date with Zeke?"

Oh, God. "Can we not talk about Zeke?"

"I second that motion," Aidan mutters.

"Hmm. Is someone jealous?" Enid sends me a knowing look across the table, earning a guffaw from Aidan.

"Of Zeke? Please."

"No, of Zeke dating Chloe."

Aidan sets his fork down, sending a scowl toward Enid's end of the table. "They're not dating."

"We aren't dating." Perhaps my admission might stop this runaway train of a conversation.

"The women in town love him," Enid interjects. It's obvious she's trying to get a rise out of her ex, and judging by his flared nostrils, it's working.

"The women in town have all had him."

Enid's blue eyes flash with mischief as she looks at me. "Is he a lousy kisser too, Chloe?"

"She wouldn't know." Thanks for that save, Aidan.

"Excuse me, Aidan, were you on the date with her?"

"We discussed our dates. It's what neighbors do. Pass the biscuits."

"I think you and Chloe should date." Natalie's statement is followed by a silence that is louder than a shotgun blast, broken only by Enid's tittering.

Aidan scrubs his face, a slight flush on his cheeks. "You have something to add?"

Enid points to herself, shaking her head. "Who, me? I would never interfere."

"Right."

Laughter flows around the table, and I'm hopeful we might change topics before Natalie asks anything else.

Natalie has other ideas. "Why aren't you two dating?" she presses, her green eyes so like her father.

"She doesn't date men with young children," Aidan blurts outs, earning a glare from me.

Oh, that's the reason? Right, because your rule has nothing to do with it.

"You love kids, Chloe." His eldest daughter is intent on getting to the bottom of things.

Might as well jump into the deep end of the pool—no lifejacket necessary.

"I do, but I dated a man for several years and helped raise his kids. Then he reconciled with his ex and took them from me. I had no say in the matter." I opt to hit Aidan with a zinger of my own. "Aidan only dates single mothers, and besides, we don't like each other like that."

A few guffaws rise from the table as the heat climbs up my face.

"Yes, you do. It's obvious. Really obvious," Natalie states, shoving some chili into her mouth.

"Are you quite done embarrassing us?" Aidan asks, sitting back in his chair. He's not angry, though, as evidenced by the smile he keeps biting back.

"No, I have tons more. I like you two together. You like her, and she likes you. What's the problem?"

And just like that, a sixteen-year-old lays our issues bare. For her, the conversation is done. She's spoken her peace, and all is right with the world.

But I feel like I showed up naked on the first day of school.

Thankfully, Jeff steps in, steering the conversation to neutral waters. I feel Aidan's gaze on me for the remainder of the meal, but I don't dare meet it.

Then he'll see that his family is correct, and I've fallen completely head over heels for him.

IT'S UNCANNY HOW QUICKLY A KITCHEN IS CLEANED when there's ample help. The flurry of activity also keeps my mind occupied, considering I don't know what will come of my relationship with Aidan now that our feelings have been made public—by everyone *but* us.

I know what I'd like to happen, but honestly, sex will only muddle everything further. Even amazing, mind-blowing sex, which I'm certain is the kind Aidan delivers.

After a ton of hugs, I'm left alone in my kitchen. Releasing a small laugh, I pull the vodka from the freezer. I need something to calm my nerves, and the wine isn't cutting it.

"Got a shot for me, too?"

Whirling around, I come face to face with Aidan, not more than three feet away. "Sure."

With trembling hands, I grasp the bottle, but Aidan has a different idea. He strides over, grabbing the bottle away.

"You don't want a shot?"

"I want you." He pulls me flush against him as he claims my mouth. When he tongues the seam of my lips, I fall into his kiss, my hands winding around his neck, desperate to get closer.

Aidan hoists me onto the counter, wrapping my legs around his waist as our mouths wage an intimate war. He tastes so good. I forgot kissing could feel this way, and when his hand knits in my hair, pulling me closer, I know he feels the same emotions.

The world falls away, leaving nothing but the two of us in this moment, our movements more desperate with each passing second. My hands grasp the front of his shirt, and his hands have since traveled down my back, cupping my ass and pressing me against his erection.

"Sorry, I forgot my bag." Emily's voice screeches into the moment, and we tear apart. "Were you two kissing?"

"No," Aidan and I reply in stereo.

"Dad, you said it's bad to lie," Emily responds, her bag in her hand. "I know you're lying because you two were definitely kissing."

On that note, she turns on her heel and walks out.

Meeting Aidan's gaze, we both burst out laughing. Covering my kiss-swollen mouth, I gaze toward the door. "Do you think she's mad?"

"No," Aidan responds. "She just thinks we're terrible liars."

"What do you think?"

"That you're the greatest kisser in the world." He ducks down, teasing his lips across mine. "I want more."

"How much more?"

"Everything, and then some." Another desperate erotic battle ensues as our tongues slide together in perfect sync. "You taste so good."

"I was thinking the same thing about you."

"Dad, Mom's car won't start. She needs a jump." This time, it's Natalie hollering from the front door.

Okay, universe, we get the hint.

Chuckling, I nod toward the entrance. "You'd better go."

Aidan nods, a wistful expression on his face. "Why do I feel like we're missing out on quite an opportunity?"

"Maybe there will be more opportunities in the future." Pressing a kiss to his mouth, I feel his breath hitch, his hands tightening around my ass. "Thank you for the flowers."

"Thank you."

"For what?"

He lifts my hand, pressing a kiss to my palm. "Being you, Chloe."

"Dad," Natalie calls again. "I have to get home and study for my test tomorrow."

"I've decided I'm disowning my children."

"Eh, I'll adopt them."

He grins, smacking a final kiss on my mouth. "You would. I'll see you later, sweets."

As the front door closes, I sag against the side of the refrigerator, reliving every delicious moment of being in Aidan's arms.

CHAPTER 9
AIDAN

I've replayed our kiss at least a million times in my mind, along with every other sexual act under the sun.

I didn't plan on kissing Chloe last night, but when she turned around, those pouty lips at the ready, there was no holding back.

Part of me figured that once I kissed her, the thrill of the unknown would fade, and we could go back to being friends with a flirtatious bent.

Not even close. Instead, the kiss upended me, feelings coursing through me the moment we touched that I've never experienced before.

Now, I want her even more than I did, which makes our situation *way* more complicated.

Seems Chloe is battling the same demons this morning, as she struggles to appear nonchalant while drinking her coffee. After a few pleasantries, she excuses herself to finish a deadline, but I notice the slight flush crawl up her cheeks when I catch her ogling my ass.

Good thing she left when she did because after she caught that sultry lower lip between her teeth, I was ready to take her straight to the bedroom.

We have our own pressing deadline.

Instead, she leaves me with my thoughts as I finish up one of the bookshelves and try not to imagine how gorgeous she looks naked.

Or how talented her tongue is on other body parts.

Not helping, Aidan.

A sudden yip stirs me from my lust-filled haze, and I look up to see Chloe in the doorway, bouncing up and down with excitement. My thoughts immediately shoot to the gutter as I notice the jiggle of her breasts under her sweatshirt.

God, I'm screwed. Or, in this case, *not* screwed.

"Good news?" I ask, trying to appear casual.

"Great news," she replies, crowding my space and assaulting my nostrils with her killer scent. I don't think she's wearing any perfume. It's just her. She's that appealing. "I was waiting to hear from this magazine about a position as a freelance feature columnist. They just called. I got it."

With an excited giggle, she throws herself into my arms, and there's no way I'm holding back. Enfolding her in my embrace, I let myself go, basking in the feel of her. "Congratulations. You deserve it. Your writing is incredible."

She pulls back, a curious expression coloring her face. "You've read my writing?"

"Guilty. I figured when you said you were a columnist that you wrote articles on sex and dating."

"Looking for some tips?" she inquires, her eyes sparkling behind her glasses. Maybe it's a coincidence, but since I mentioned my fondness for the sexy librarian look, she wears her glasses more. I keep telling myself it's for my benefit.

Either way, she's gorgeous.

I lean in, my mouth hovering mere inches from hers. "No, I'm a master in that arena."

"Do you have any credentials to back up that claim?"

"I can provide hands-on experience." Holy shit, I'm one second away from ripping her clothes off to show her how talented I am at giving her pleasure.

Like I said, I bet she's a screamer, and I'm dying to find out.

"I'm sure you have a long list of satisfied clients," she quips, tapping a finger against her mouth and once again drawing attention to her perfect lips.

Her perfectly kissable lips.

She tasted so good.

I need to focus before I lose the last of my willpower, and trust me, it's hanging by a thread.

As if sensing my internal dilemma, Chloe steps away, motioning to the piles of wood and tools. "Forget all this and come celebrate with me."

"Now?" Granted, I've put in a full day already. Plus, I'm curious to know what kind of celebration she has in mind.

"Seems as good a time as any. I'll help you clean up, and we can have a celebratory dinner." She pauses, shooting me a coy smirk. "Take it from there."

Yes, please. A million times would be preferable.

Then I groan, and it isn't from anticipation. "Crap, I can't tonight. I'm playing."

Her brow furrows. "Playing?"

"Me and a couple of guys have a band. Nothing fancy—a handful of originals, mostly covers—but we play down at the bar every Thursday."

Chloe bites her lip again, nodding absently. "Huh."

"Come with me." Actually, I'd love to show her off to the

guys while also sending a message to good old Zeke to back off. I know him, and once he's got his hooks in a woman, he hates to let go.

I heard through the grapevine that he's very interested in another date with Chloe, and I'm intent on showing him how sorry he'll be if he pursues that path.

"Like a date?"

"Date." My mind tries on the word like a pair of leather pants—odd at first but strangely comfortable. "Uh, sure."

Now she's blushing, shaking her hands as if to clear away her question. "Why did I say that? I know it's not a date. That wasn't how I meant it."

Her words say one thing, but her face assures me she meant her original question. Again, something that makes me strangely comfortable. "How about we'll be two people going out together to have a drink and listen to some fantastic music courtesy of me?"

"Fantastic, huh?" she giggles.

"I have to work the self-promotion angle. Come on, Chloe. You might have fun." And after I'm done playing, we'll *both* have fun.

She frowns at her leggings. "This involves putting on pants."

"Generally, although I've seen some natives buck the trend. Besides, you wanted to go out to dinner. You'd have to put on pants then, too."

She considers my statement. "I don't know. It's not that I don't want to hear you play, but I'm not really an 'up all night' kind of girl anymore."

"You won't be. We finish early, and I'll have you back in bed before midnight."

I thought the sexual tension was bad before? My dick is throbbing at this point.

"You think you're that good, huh?"

"I think I can be. I guess you have to see firsthand."

"Or I could ask your long line of satisfied customers."

"I much prefer my scenario."

There's that sex kitten smile again. The best part? It's unintentional, but it still makes me want to bend her over the counter and show her how satisfied she can be. "Your way is far too dangerous, Aidan."

"But far more fun."

"True." She grabs another cup of coffee, leaning against the doorframe as her eyes rove over my body. "Why not? I'll put on pants like a normal human and meet you there. Deal?"

That would be the easiest way to handle the situation, mainly since there's a good chance Barbara will show up tonight. But I want to arrive with Chloe on my arm, not as my buddy cheering me on from a bar stool. "I'll drive you. That way, you can't escape midway through the first song."

"When you said fantastic, you actually mean ear-screeching!"

"Don't you know those terms are interchangeable?"

"I don't want to kill your flow with the ladies."

The second she tosses out that idea, I rush to dead it. "Chloe, what kind of guy would I be if I hit on other women while I was out with you?"

"A single one."

"A single one on a date. I'm not like that."

"I thought it wasn't a date." Now those dark eyes bore holes into me, daring me to worm my way out, back away from the whole concept.

Not happening, Chloe, because, at that moment, I realize a date is the only thing I want it to be.

She winks, nodding at the clock. "Time to make myself

presentable. You sure you don't mind picking me up? I am out of the way, after all."

Just like that, she eases us back into our usual, comfortable banter. Away from the heavy innuendos and lingering desire.

But unlike before, when I'd be grateful for the diversion, I'm tired of denying what I feel for her. Tired of convincing myself that feeling something for her is wrong.

Tired of my damn rules.

I created them, so I should be able to break the damn things.

I SPEND *WAY* TOO MUCH TIME GETTING READY FOR OUR non-date, even getting a haircut and professional shave.

Holy crap, I have it bad.

After trying on three shirts, I grunt in disgust, realizing this is what it's like to be a woman. Every. Damn. Day.

I finally settle on a pair of jeans and a black t-shirt. It's classic. Simple.

Doesn't look like I'm trying too hard.

I contemplate getting Chloe flowers again but realize that's muddying up already turgid waters.

It's just two friends going to the local bar, where she can watch my band play.

Two friends who kissed last night.

Two friends who desperately want to sleep together.

Two friends who know that sleeping together is likely a terrible idea for said friendship.

Do I still want to sleep with Chloe? You better believe it.

I'm on her doorstep at eight o'clock, trying my best to appear natural.

It's not a date. It's not a date.

"Why did you ring the bell? You have a key." She pauses, looking up at me. "Nice haircut."

"Thanks. Figured I needed a different style for the whole no beard look."

"You look fantastic. Now you're making me feel like a slacker."

She sure doesn't look like one. Most days, Chloe dresses for comfort, which makes sense since she works from home.

But I got an eyeful—and a handful—of her luscious body last night, and all I can say is she's got the most incredible ass on the damn planet.

Judging by the skintight pants she's wearing, she knows it.

There's no hiding a single curve under the gray fabric, and when she bends over to turn on a table lamp, I notice something else. She's not wearing underwear.

I get it's likely a fashion choice and not a subtle hint toward playtime, but my dick doesn't care. It's all systems go, and we haven't even left the house yet.

"You look amazing, Chloe."

She does, too. Besides the pants, she's got on a sweater that slips off one shoulder, offering a hint of the most kissable skin I've ever seen.

In other words? If Zeke takes one step toward Chloe tonight, I'm knocking him on his ass.

The pub sits on the outskirts of town, but it has ample parking and an enormous beer selection. It's a local haunt, not trendy, like the tourist traps lining the main streets.

We walk in and order a drink, but I notice the stares. One, I look *way* different than I did a couple of weeks ago, and two, Chloe doesn't blend in with the local population—in a good way. A *very* good way.

Carl and Jack, two of the guys in the band, are already here, and they waste no time giving me shit about my appearance.

"Look at the pretty boy," Carl says, sidling up next to me at the bar, a smirk on his face.

"Just because I shaved and got a haircut doesn't make me a damn pretty boy." I watch as Chloe disappears into the bathroom, eyes following her the entire way.

"Let me guess, is it because of her? She's gorgeous, by the way. Who is that?"

"Remember Betsey? That's her daughter."

Carl's eyes widen. "I thought you hated her."

I shrug, swigging back my beer. "Turns out I don't. I had her pegged wrong."

Carl gives me an elbow in the ribs, an evil gleam in his eye. "I'll bet you want to peg her in all the wrong ways."

Usually, I tolerate the sexist banter, but I don't appreciate anyone speaking that way about Chloe. "Don't be an asshole."

"I met her the other day," Jack pipes in. "She's really nice." He's the peacemaker of the band, and once again, he's on duty.

"I'll bet." Carl stalks off, muttering about the soundcheck.

"What's his issue?" I ask Jack.

"His old lady caught him with Helen again, and she's been making his life hell ever since."

"She should." Here's the thing. I don't abide cheating. I fully understand that you can date several people simultaneously, so long as *all* parties are on the same page. But once you speak those vows? That's a different story. That's a commitment, not something you follow when you feel like it.

"Want to play pool?" Jack asks, nodding toward the table.

"Can we?" Chloe asks over my shoulder.

Swiveling on the bar stool, I smile. Hell, I always smile when

Chloe is around, and now, her dark eyes sparkle with excitement. "You like pool?"

She nods, tonguing her lower lip and once again sending my mind to the gutter. "I'm not any good, but there's only one way to improve, right?"

"Good point."

Besides, how bad can she be?

Five minutes later, I have my answer. She's terrible, but she's also adorable. Thankfully, Jack finds the entire situation amusing and is letting me act as Chloe's unofficial coach in an attempt for her to sink something.

Anything at this point is an improvement.

"Chloe, come here." I wave her over to me, noticing her embarrassed grin.

"Here," she hands me the pool cue. "I'm worse than I remember, and I didn't think that was possible."

"Let me give you a couple of pointers." I wrap my arms around her, my hands resting over hers as they grasp the cue.

Bad idea. A very bad idea that feels so very good.

Her ass.

My cock.

What the hell was I doing again?

Through some miracle, I focus long enough to get off a shot, and her ball teeters before dropping in the pocket.

Chloe releases the pool cue, an excited yelp coming from her lips as she claps her hands.

I step back, but she turns, hands on hips and a come-hither expression on her face. "That's it? One and done?"

No, sweets, it will last all night. You have my word.

I catch Jack's grin at our openly flirtatious display. "I'm going to set up. You two finish it out."

Thanks, man, I owe you one.

"You want more lessons?" I ask Chloe, loving the way my heady stare seems to unhinge her.

"Only if you're offering."

I wrap my arms around her again, but this time, I don't give a damn what ball she aims for. I know what *I'm* aiming for—her affections. Pushing her long hair over one shoulder, I nuzzle her neck, hearing her breath hitch. "You smell good."

She smiles, but I can tell she's desperately trying to appear unaffected. "Eau de pool hall, with the faint underpinnings of beer."

"My favorite scent." I adore this smart ass.

She chuckles before returning her focus to the game, intent on the task at hand.

But we have two different outcomes. She wants to learn how to play pool, and I want to learn how to play her.

I drift my lips along the column of her neck, barely dusting her skin. But it's enough. It's more than enough. Her entire body clenches at my subtle exploration, her breathing shallow and heated. "Best smelling beer ever."

"Amber," she manages, her voice soft. "It's amber."

"No, Chloe. It's you."

"Maybe it's just what I do to you."

That's it. I don't give a damn how many people are here. I want to bend her over this table and sink inside her until tomorrow morning. "You have no idea."

"Aidan, care to join us, or are you too busy with the beautiful lady?"

Glancing up, I see Carl motioning to the stage. Playtime is over.

"Time to go to work."

"I can't wait to see you play," she exclaims, pressing a kiss to my cheek.

I can't wait to play you, sweets.

※

I never told Chloe what instrument I play, but she's obviously impressed when I take my place at the front of the stage. Perhaps if I hadn't rushed off to get married, I would have pursued a career in music, but now, it's a way to blow off steam and a hell of a good way to garner attention from the ladies.

The only difference is now I'm only concerned about *one* lady.

Our band plays a good mix of rock-and-roll covers, with a few of my originals thrown in. Each member is solid, and my voice attracts women like moths to a flame.

As I scan the audience, I notice Barbara has arrived, and luckily, she isn't alone. I know she hoped something would grow from our dinner date, but I felt nothing with her.

Unlike with Chloe, where I feel everything.

Judging from the way Barbara is hanging on her date, she's determined to show me how little our time together meant, but I'm okay with that. Actually, I'm thrilled she moved on so quickly.

Now I can focus on the one woman who usurps my every thought. A woman who also has the greatest hip shake I've ever seen.

Seems many of the bar patrons agree, their eyes glued to Chloe's body as she sways to the beat. Some women have a natural grace, an ability to work their bodies in a hypnotic subliminal call.

Chloe is the best I've ever seen, those wide hips and round ass gyrating on the floor until I'm certain every guy in the place has a hard-on.

She's not even trying to draw attention to herself. If anything, she's lost in me, her dark gaze focused on my every move.

Talk about an ego boost and a half.

When we take a break, I make a beeline for Chloe. Time to stake my claim before one of a dozen men come any closer.

She pulls me into a hug, her face glowing with excitement.

"Did you like it?"

"Loved it," she exclaims. "You are so talented, Aidan. I don't know how much you can see under those lights, but I was a dancing fool."

"I saw. You've got some moves. I might have to set a perimeter around you, though."

Her smile falters. "Am I that spastic?"

"No, but every guy in the bar was drooling in your direction."

"How do you know?"

"I saw them, and I didn't like it."

"Are you feeling overprotective?"

"We'll go with that term, sure."

"I didn't notice anyone looking at me. Then again, I was focused on you. You were hot as hell up there. Granted, you're always hot at hell."

I'm not sure if it's the liquor loosening her lips, but I don't care. It's all systems go. "Trust me, they all stripped you naked in their minds. Like I said, you can move."

Chloe gives her ass a smack, and I'm tempted to let her know I'll take over that job for her. "How can I not, with an ass like this?"

Exactly.

Thank Christ, I didn't say that out loud.

"No matter what I do—diet and exercise—I can't ever lose the ass."

"Stop trying."

"Are you saying you like my ass?"

"Like would be an understatement, but I'm a gentleman."

Rising on tiptoe, she hovers her mouth mere inches from mine. "And if you weren't a gentleman?"

This woman. Holy shit. She's got me tied up in knots and horny as hell, all in the same breath. I lean down, my lips caressing her ear as my hand slides down to cup the curve of her ass. "I would pay our tab, take you home, peel off those jeans, bend you over my table and show you how delectable I think your ass is." When I hear her sexy little gasp, I know I've got her. With a light smack, I straighten up, offering her a wink. "But, I'm a gentleman."

"Huh."

"What?"

"I'm wondering what the full range of your personal attention looks like."

To be fair, she started it. But I'm sure as hell going to finish it. Backing Chloe against the wall, I cage her in, my forearms resting on either side of her head. "I'll lick every inch of you until you're screaming my name, and the only thought you'll have in your head from that point on is how good my tongue feels wrapped around your clit."

The air is thick with desire as the energy sparks between us. Her pupils dilate as a faint sheen of sweat breaks across her brow. Oh, yes, that did it.

I take a step back before I make good on my promise in front of the entire bar. Would I go down on her right here?

Hell, yes, I would.

"Cat got your tongue, Chloe?"

She runs her hands under her hair before pivoting to show off that gorgeous rear. "I was just thinking what a shame it is that you're a man of morals. I sure could go for some personal attention."

My cock springs to attention, damn near busting out of my jeans. It's like a homing device, aiming straight for what lies between Chloe's thighs.

Her gaze drops to my pants before meeting my hooded stare. "Granted, I'd expect equal time. You can't have all the fun. Have a good second set, handsome."

"Holy fuck," I mutter as she struts away, those hips swaying in a nonverbal call to me.

"Who is that hot commodity?"

"Back off, Darryl," I bark to the drummer, my eyes glued to Chloe's retreating form.

"I guess she's taken."

"Damn straight."

By the time I pull into my driveway later that night, I know two things.

I'm desperate for Chloe, and I'm falling desperately in love with her.

The first concept I can handle. The other one scares the shit out of me.

To top it off, my phone has gone off five times since we left the bar, and it isn't Enid or the girls.

It's Barbara. She cornered me after the second set, obviously in her cups, and terribly upset that I was with another woman. The fact she was with another man seemed to slip her mind, but I wanted to be the good guy. I spent ten minutes consoling her, and when I walked back over to Chloe, I knew she'd seen the interaction.

Like a true lady, Chloe said nothing, but the levity of earlier in the evening was gone.

Time to get things back on track. I walk Chloe to her door as I silence yet another call.

"Is she okay?"

"I'm sure she's fine."

She unlocks the door, turning toward me, a smile on her sexy mouth. "Do you want to come inside?"

"Yes."

No sooner has the word left my mouth than my phone rings again. "That's it, I'm changing my number."

"Answer the phone," Chloe instructs. "It might be important."

"I'm sure it isn't."

"Do it, anyway."

With a grunt, I accept the call. "Hey Barbara, what's up?"

"Aidan, my date bailed, and I'm really drunk. Can you please come to get me?"

"I just got home. Can't someone else take you?"

Chloe touches my arm, and I meet her gaze.

"Hang on, Barbara."

"Go," Chloe mouths.

"I don't want to," I hiss back. Is she insane? The *only* thing I want is to admire every inch of Chloe for the rest of the night. Hear her scream my name as I make her come again and again.

Barbara doesn't figure at *all* into this scenario.

Unfortunately, Chloe won't be deterred. "She's drunk and alone at a bar with men who can and will take advantage. If you don't go, I will, even though I shouldn't be driving."

I groan, putting the phone back to my ear. "I'll be there in ten minutes." Ending the call, I motion to the truck. "Why don't you come with me?"

"That's a bad idea. She really likes you, Aidan. I think tonight was hard on her."

"She was with another guy," I argue, considering it's a totally valid point.

"To make you jealous. Now she's upset and drunk and will have a terrible hangover tomorrow. You're a good man. Go do the right thing."

"I thought I was," I mutter as Chloe kisses my cheek. "I want to spend tonight with you."

"Maybe the universe is trying to tell us something."

"Yes, that I need to change my number. I guess by the time I finish dropping Barbara off, you'll be asleep, right?"

She nods, and I release another groan. "Goodnight, Aidan. You were spectacular tonight."

I stall on Chloe's stoop, even after she's walked inside.

I want to be with Chloe.

I'm tired of being the good guy.

The guy with the rules.

The guy *without* the woman he's falling in love with.

CHAPTER 10
CHLOE

I made a decision after our outing to the bar. I'm not pursuing Aidan.

It's not that I don't want to, because my heart is seriously tangled up in the man, but this will end badly.

He and I want different things, and even if we got past that hurdle, there's always the fact that I don't fit his rule. Barbara does.

Plus, I still want a baby, and I *know* that's not on his radar.

Too many variables, adding up to one answer—Aidan and I are a bad idea.

He didn't show up for work at the house the next day, claiming a townsperson had an emergency repair.

Was he lying? I don't know, and it wasn't my place to ask.

In a way, it's easier if he gives Barbara a second chance. She seems like a lovely woman, outside of the fact she isn't too crazy about me, but who can blame her? I'm the goalie blocking the net.

With me out of the way, she'll score easily.

See? All sewn up, nice and neat, and I'll keep repeating it in my head until I believe the load of crap I just created.

I know what Aidan wanted that night. I wanted the same thing, and if I had opened the door, we would have spent the night pleasuring each other, and no doubt, it would have been magnificent.

But what then? The slow, painful torture of watching a friendship dissolve because we crossed a perimeter we should have heeded?

There is no easy answer.

No matter what, I have to see him tonight. It's Enid's birthday party, down at the local VFW hall. I know he'll be there, and I'm certain Barbara will, too. The question is whether they arrive together.

Actually, the more important question is whether they *leave* together.

Again, not my business, but that won't stop my brain from ruminating on the possibilities.

I arrive a bit early, per Enid's request. She asked if I would help her decorate, and there is no way I'll let her down. Besides, she shouldn't be decorating for her *own* party.

But I'm troubled. Something is off with Enid, although I can't put my finger on exactly what. She looks exhausted, although having three kids will enhance the bags under your eyes, particularly since Natalie has a new obsession. I don't know what his name is yet, but no doubt she'll tell me before the night is through.

Per Enid, it's all Natalie can talk about. Good old teenage angst.

Turns out they also called Aidan in early to the festivities, and he's busy setting up the stage for his band to play. Thankfully,

Barbara is nowhere to be found—yet—but several other women are making their desires *very* obvious where Aidan is concerned.

"Vultures," Enid mutters, following my gaze. "He's turned them all down at least a dozen times, but that doesn't stop them from trying."

"He's a good-looking, successful man who also happens to be a nice guy. I'm not surprised they're trying."

Enid fixes me with her blue glare. "That's just it. Why aren't you trying? You two have a thing for one another."

I shake my head, maintaining my focus on the streamers in my hand. "We have a flirtation, but that's all. We're friends —*good* friends—, and we don't want to mess up that connection. Sex complicates things. It muddies the waters. Our friendship is important to me, and I don't want to ruin it. I never want Aidan to regret the idea of me."

Okay, I didn't mean to verbally vomit my heart onto Enid, but it's too late now.

A knowing smile crosses her face as she hangs some light catchers. "Are you trying to convince yourself or me?"

"Both," I manage.

"Some of the world's greatest love affairs are born from friendship. Remember that." She motions toward the stage. "Do me a favor? Let Aidan know he better play my favorite song tonight."

"Why don't you tell him? You carry far more clout."

"Because," she adds with a wink, "you obviously need a reason to speak to him since you're both too chickenshit to do it on your own."

Enid stumbles as she steps onto the ladder, and I grab her arm. "Sit down. I'll go up on the ladder." Climbing to the top, I lean forward, stealing another glance toward Aidan, surrounded by a few *different* women this time. Grr. "Enid, can I ask you something?"

"Yes, you should absolutely pursue Aidan."

"Not even remotely what I planned to ask. Are you okay? You seem tired lately."

"I can't seem to shake this cold."

"Have you seen a doctor?"

She nods, averting her gaze. "So far, everything looks normal. She figures I'm entering menopause early. Lucky me, right? So much for having a baby with Jeff."

I pause at her words. "I didn't realize you two were considering that."

"He's never asked, but I'd love to have a baby with him, and I think he'd enjoy having a child of his own."

"I figured you wouldn't want more, since you have three kids already."

She shrugs, handing me another light catcher. "I don't have one with Jeff."

"What a love story, Enid."

It's true. Something about the simplicity of her statement simultaneously warms and hurts my heart.

If only I could find someone like that, who would want to explore life together, then I wouldn't have to consider being inseminated with a stranger's sperm.

Regardless of how my baby is created, I know one thing. He will be loved. Of that, I'm certain.

"You know," Enid sends me a mock scowl, "you could have that great love story, too. But you have to stop stalling. Go on, I know you want to talk to him."

With a sigh, I drop the streamers on the table and head across the room to where Aidan sits, tuning his guitar. He has such effortless good looks, and right now, with his tousled hair and day-old stubble littering his cheeks, he's downright scrumptious.

"Hey, there." At least my voice sounds normal. Score one for the home team.

Aidan glances up, a smile crossing his face, those dimples at the ready. "Hey, yourself. Where have you been? I tried calling you, but you didn't answer."

I shrug, well aware of the missed calls. "I'm sorry about that. I was under the gun for a deadline."

"I was worried. That, and I missed you." He nods toward Enid, a furrow crossing his brow. "Can I ask you something?"

"Sure."

"Have you noticed anything off with Enid? You two are close, and I thought maybe she had said something."

"I asked her about it today, and she said she can't shake this cold. Her doctor mentioned something about entering menopause."

"She's only thirty-nine."

"It happens sometimes. Hopefully, it's an easy fix." My gaze falls on my friend as Jeff swings her into his arms. "I love their love."

Immediately, I regret speaking those words aloud, especially to Aidan. "I'm sorry, I wasn't thinking."

Aidan chuckles before returning his attention to his guitar. "I love their love, too. I envy it, sometimes. Not because I want Enid back—we're far better as friends—but because they have such a deep and passionate affection for each other."

"You have your choice of women in this town. I saw at least six vying for your affection."

Aidan fixes me with his emerald gaze. "The only trouble? I don't want them."

"Too bad for them, I suppose."

"Is it, really?"

Hello flush, good to see you again. "I have to finish with the... the decorations. Oh, Enid says you better play her favorite song, or she'll hunt you down."

I throw in the last bit for effect, but judging by the amused smile on Aidan's face, it works.

"I'll consider her request, but only if you dance for me tonight."

"We'll see. Anything is possible."

I'M TORN.

I'm fully aware the friend zone is safer for both Aidan and me, but I want to claw out the eyes of every woman making a play for his attention.

It's not Aidan's fault. He's sexy without trying, especially with that gravelly voice and those deft fingers moving over the frets. Proof of how talented his mouth and hands are without even touching a woman.

So, to avoid jealousy overload, I plant myself in the back, and people watch. It's always been a favorite activity of mine, and there is no shortage of interesting subjects at this party—particularly Natalie and her crush.

Ah, young love.

"Are you going to let those women hang on my dad?"

I turn, my eyes widening as Natalie plops down beside me. "What?"

"You want my father, and if you want something, you have to claim it."

"You're telling me to claim your father?"

"Yep," Natalie nods, her eyes focused on the stage. "He has a thing for you, but you already know that."

"He doesn't date women without kids."

"He doesn't date."

"Even better—insurmountable odds." I pivot in my chair, nodding toward Natalie's crush. "What's his name?"

"Jason. He's a football player on the varsity team."

"Nice. He's good-looking."

"He knows it."

I grimace. "Don't tell me he's one of *those* guys."

Natalie giggles. "Not really, although he has his moments. He said he wants to take me to dinner. He'll pay and everything."

"He better pay, or I'll have a word with him."

"What should I do? How do I act?"

"You don't *ever* act. That's too hard to maintain. Be yourself, and if he's got a brain in his head, he'll like you for who you *really* are. Trust me on this."

Natalie stands, giving me a hug. "Trust *me* on my father."

If only adult relationships were as straightforward as puppy love.

Sadly, love only gets more challenging to navigate as the years pass.

I wander into an empty side room, grinning when I see the pool table. I love playing pool, even though I'm the worst player on the face of the planet.

At least now, I can play with no one making fun of me. It won't be as much fun as when Aidan gave me a lesson, but it's far safer for my heart and all my other body parts.

I know I can do this. How hard can it be?

Answer?

Much too hard for me, as evidenced by my inability to sink anything.

"Snuck off to practice, huh?"

I glance over my shoulder to where Aidan stands, arms crossed over his chest, a bemused grin on his face.

"In about a million more years, I might be decent." Missing again, I toss down the pool cue. "Or not."

Aidan strolls over, picking up the pool cue and sinking a ball. Damn him for making it look effortless. Why does he have to be good at *everything*? "You might not win any billiards tournaments, but you're incredible at so many other things."

"You guys sound fantastic tonight."

"I kept waiting for my favorite dancer to take the floor, but she never showed."

"Sitting this one out," I reply, pushing my glasses up my nose. Yes, I downplayed my looks tonight. What's the point? At least I'm *not* wearing leggings.

"Come here, my sexy librarian." Aidan motions me to his side, handing me the pool cue and wrapping his arms around me. "I have my own theory about your pool playing abilities."

Desperate to remain centered, I focus on the table, trying to gauge if I have a shot. "That one?"

"Sure," Aidan murmurs, his mouth close to my ear. "My theory is you're shooting like crap, hoping to get extra lessons."

I snort at his egotistical insinuation, even if it's right on the money. But hey, he doesn't have to know that fact. "I think you're giving extra lessons to get up close and personal with my ass, cowboy."

A deep chuckle rises from his chest. "I think you're right."

"I think we both are." Wriggling ever so slightly, I hear his breath hitch, his grip tightening around me.

"You'd better behave, Chloe."

I tease him with another shake of my assets, just for fun.

"My ass has never been good at behaving. Besides, I'm

responsible for the balls in front of me. You're responsible for the ones behind me."

"Might work better if we switched that around." Just like that, Aidan takes back control of the banter.

But tonight, I'm fighting him for the crown.

I stretch back against him. To an outsider, it's barely noticeable. But for us, it's stoking an already smoldering fire.

The delicious prickle of his stubble moves across my neck, his lips hovering centimeters from my ear. "Focus, sweets."

"Hard to focus when your mouth is so close to my neck." I know I'm pushing it, testing the limits. Testing *our* limits.

His teeth scrape against my throat, soothed by the gentle lash of his tongue. "Would you like me to pick a different spot?"

"How accommodating of you," I manage, my heart racing.

"I prefer to think of myself as multi-talented."

I search my brain for a quick-witted retort, struggling to regain equal footing with Aidan. Not happening.

As if sensing my internal battle, he removes his hands from the pool cue, curling his fingers around my hips. He presses against me, his erection straining against those sexy-as-fuck jeans, and I bite back a moan as my head drops back against his chest.

We should stop. I know it. He knows it. But our bodies demand to be satiated. To be fed.

"I wish we were alone." Holy shit. Did I say that aloud?

His fingers tighten as he locks me between the pool table and his muscled frame. "You have no idea what you do to me. You are the ultimate aphrodisiac, Chloe."

All I can manage is a low moan, my body teetering on the brink of self-control.

He rains kisses along the column of my throat as I reach

behind me, scratching my nails down his thighs. "I wanted to stay with you that night. Why did you send me away?"

"You needed to take care of Barbara."

"I needed to take care of you. I needed to take care of us. I'm going out of my mind, just being near you. You're so beautiful, and you have no idea how much I want you."

"Are you kidding? I look like a mess tonight."

"You're gorgeous." He nips my ear as his fingers drift around my waist to play with the button on my jeans. With a flick, he pops it open, and my breath catches.

He won't actually do anything here, with everyone gathered in the next room. He can't.

Until he does.

Aidan slides a hand past my waistband, stroking along my slick skin before plunging his fingers inside me.

A soft moan falls from my lips as his fingers work me over, making me ache.

Emotions flood through me, but Aidan isn't stopping, determined to bring me the pleasure I denied us both the other night.

"Aidan," I whisper, writhing against his hand. The more I squirm, the tighter his grip becomes, holding me in the moment until he's damn well ready to let me go. When his thumb brushes across my clit, it's all over.

I shatter, my knees buckling as his muscular arms hold me steady.

He slides his fingers from my pants, curling his tongue around them before delivering a gentle bite to my shoulder.

"You're delectable, but I want all of you, Chloe." Aidan spins me around as his mouth claims mine, his movements possessive and so, so delicious.

His hands slide under my sweater, creeping up to tease the

bottom of my bra as his mouth whispers of my every sensual pleasure fulfilled. If only I'll let him.

I desperately want to allow him to have free rein over my body, and judging by the trembling beneath his skin, he needs me just as much.

"Why can't I stay away from you?" I whisper, tracing my fingers along his mouth.

"Maybe we need to ask why we keep trying instead."

Someone coughs behind us, and we turn to see Enid in the doorway, barely containing her laughter. "I hate to break up this private party, but I need you two for birthday cake."

"Sure. Aidan was teaching me—"

"Oh, I *know* what he was teaching you. Seems you're an A+ student," she smirks.

"Oh, my God," I mumble, my cheeks flaming.

Finally, her laugh escapes, rising into the air, along with my mortification. "Hey, I'm thrilled. It's about damn time."

"But we aren't..." I trail off, catching Aidan's bemused expression.

So glad everyone finds this situation amusing.

Me? I fall somewhere between confused and horny as hell, despite the incredible orgasm Aidan gifted me.

What can I say? I want more.

Glancing at Aidan, I meet his soft gaze as he holds out his hand. "Come on. They're waiting on us."

It's a simple gesture, but I know it screams volumes for a man like Aidan. He's openly flirtatious but openly affectionate? That's a different story.

With a smile, I slide my hand into his, feeling the warmth flow through my body. When his fingers tighten around mine, I realize my heart doesn't stand a chance.

I'm lost to this man.

CHAPTER 11
AIDAN

"Leave me alone, Dad," Natalie wails, slamming the front door, her face red from crying.

"What the hell happened?" I ask, throwing up my hands in resignation.

I can't figure it out. Everything was fine last night at the party—better than fine. Natalie was all smiles as she chatted up the boy she likes. Enid danced the night away with Emily and Mia. And Chloe… Chloe was perfect.

She was as tight and wet as I knew she would be, which made sleeping alone that much more difficult. Enid and Jeff offered to take the girls, but they had a private weekend planned. One without our children. No matter how much my dick hated me, and it did, I wasn't taking that time away from them—although it was a tempting thought when Enid giggled about my pressing sexual needs.

The woman knows me better than anyone. Hell, she knew I'd fallen for Chloe even before *I* was aware of the fact.

Any chance of me spending the night loving on Chloe's naked body was ixnayed so I could look after the girls.

I adore my girls, but damn, I wish I was childless last night.

Sunday started out perfect—sunny and crisp with hot coffee and my two youngest being their usual silly selves—until Natalie burst through the door in the early afternoon, demanding I leave her alone.

"Teenagers," I mutter, running a hand through my hair.

"Is everything okay?"

Turning, I smile at Chloe, wrapped in yet another blanket as she stands on her porch, water in hand.

God, I love this woman.

The thought hits me hard and fast, but for the first time, I don't run from it. Instead, I invite it into my heart and let it stay.

Now, I have to convince Chloe to stay, too. Convince her of all the reasons why life here is superior to any existence in the big city. No simple task, but I'm ready to take it on as soon as I get to the bottom of the Natalie mystery.

"Natalie just rushed inside, all upset. She's mad at... who knows who she's mad at? She isn't speaking to anyone. Certainly not me."

Chloe is off her porch, heading toward my house. "Was she out with Jason earlier?"

Chances are, Chloe knows more about this guy than I do.

"Yeah. They went ice-skating."

"Can I go in and speak with her?"

"Be my guest," I reply, motioning to the house.

Women. I'll never be able to figure them out, and yet, I'm surrounded by them.

Here's the thing. I adore my daughters more than life itself, but I always wanted a little boy running around the house. Someone to take fishing and four-wheeling while instilling all that fatherly advice my old man never bothered to share with me. A do-over of sorts, with the father and son bond.

I make sure my daughters know they're my world. Growing up without parental bonds taught me how important they are—the scars of neglect last a lifetime. I'm far from perfect, but I always do my best. They deserve my best—every damn day.

I wander into the kitchen, noting that it's eerily quiet upstairs. At least Natalie isn't chucking stuff across the room—something to be thankful for.

"I'm stealing her for the night."

Looking up, I see Chloe, her arm wrapped around Natalie. My daughter's face is stained with tears, but she manages a sad smile in my direction. Natalie may be a few inches taller than Chloe, but Chloe emits a sense of strength and security.

She makes my girls feel safe. I'm indebted to her for that and so much more.

"Is everything okay?"

"Go get your stuff ready, and let me talk to your dad."

Natalie nods, walking into the other room.

"Boy trouble," Chloe explains, a rueful smile on her lips. "She's going to be fine, but she needs some girl time."

"Thank you for helping her. Are you sure you don't mind?" I flash Chloe a smile, realizing how I'm always smiling around Chloe.

Hell, I'm always smiling just *thinking* about Chloe.

"You don't have to thank me. That girl in there? I'm crazy about her."

Suddenly, I can't hold back the emotions anymore. They're too overwhelming, feelings that have simmered for the last several weeks. Pulling Chloe close, I push her dark hair from her ear, letting my mouth nuzzle her skin. "This girl right here? I'm crazy about her, too."

At dinnertime, I order Mexican food instead of cooking. First, I'm hardly a chef, and second, Mexican is Natalie's favorite.

The restaurant sits in a strip mall, next to a family-owned jewelry store. Usually, I pay the place no mind as I dash in to grab my order, but today, I step inside. I enjoy surprising my girls with gifts when they least expect them, and after the day Natalie has had, perhaps something from here might make her smile.

Five minutes later, the clerk wraps up a ruby necklace. Red is Nat's favorite color, plus she was born in July. Hopefully, this helps ease the pain of boy trouble. I could also kick Jason's ass, but that would be *way* more fun for me, considering he made my daughter cry.

"Will that be all, sir?" the jeweler asks as he ties a bow around the box.

My eyes drift to the case, to a gold choker that caught my eye the minute I walked in. It's not Natalie's taste, but I know someone who would love it.

Someone who, as far as I can tell, rarely gets gifts.

"I'll take that choker, as well."

When I hop back in my truck, I'm several hundred dollars poorer, but if it makes either of them happy, it's worth every penny.

Once my two youngest are chowing down on burritos, I walk next door to drop off their dinner and surprise gifts.

Chloe opens the door, and I damn near drop the bag of food. She's wearing a dark green face mask and a towel on her head. She looks absolutely ridiculous, and I tell her so in between laughs.

Thankfully, she's a good sport, giggling as she waves me

inside. "It made Natalie laugh, so I consider it a win. That you are *also* amused is a bonus. Give me a second to peel this gunk off my face."

She's back a moment later, looking fresh-faced with her hair bouncing around her shoulders. It must be something to do with that green crap.

"How's Nat doing?"

"Better. I placated her with a hot fudge sundae before telling her that most men are complete idiots. I told her that's why God invented chocolate."

"Most men are morons. A sad fact, isn't it?"

"There are some good guys out there. I informed Natalie that she should strive for a man like you, even though you're a rarity."

My heart catches at Chloe's words. "You didn't say that."

"Right hand to God."

"Thank you... for believing I'm a good man." Truth is, it may be the greatest compliment anyone has ever paid me.

"I don't believe it, Aidan. I know it for a fact."

Those overwhelming feelings? Taken on a whole new level after this chat.

"Hey, Dad."

Turning, I pull Natalie into a hug, snickering at her purple face mask. "It's a good look, Nat. You should consider this for everyday wear."

"Start a new trend," she giggles.

"I brought you two Mexican food, and," I reach into my pocket, pulling out the necklace, "I got you this. I know it's just from your old man, but I thought it might make you smile."

Natalie opens the box, a grin splitting her face. "It's a ruby. Thank you, Dad." She buries her head in my chest, and I glance at Chloe, who is all smiles, sending me a thumbs up.

Natalie shows Chloe the necklace, and Chloe wastes no time helping her put it on. "That is absolutely stunning. The way it sets off the dark purple of the mask—"

My eldest daughter pulls Chloe into a hug, and I see how Chloe's touch warms her soul. The woman is a gift for us all.

"Go clean up, and I'm going to fix us some enormous plates of food before our movie marathon." Chloe inhales deeply, releasing a sigh. "It smells amazing. Thank you for dinner, Aidan, but more importantly, thank you for being the good guy she needs right now."

How does she always know the right thing to say? Every sentiment shoots straight into my heart, lodging there as a permanent reminder of the woman who haunts my dreams.

"Wait. I got you something, too."

"Extra habanero salsa?" Chloe asks with a grin.

"That's in the bag, but I saw this and couldn't resist." I pull out the box, my heart clenching as her eyes widen in surprise.

"For me? But why?" Chloe still hasn't touched the box, but her expression breaks my heart. I was right. She probably hasn't gotten a gift since she lost her father at eighteen.

"Sometimes, the best reason is no reason at all."

Natalie's eyes brighten as she returns to the room. "Open it, Chloe."

With trembling fingers, Chloe opens the box, her hand flying to her mouth as she looks at the choker.

"If it's not something you like, I can exchange it."

But when she looks up, her eyes are filled with tears. "It's gorgeous, Aidan. I don't deserve this."

"You deserve way the hell more than a gold necklace."

Chloe throws her arms around me, and this time, I get a thumbs up of approval from Natalie. Seems my entire family is hell-bent on the two of us getting together, and I see now they were right all along.

Chloe makes me happy. Making her happy makes me happy.

I never planned on her, but now that she's here, I know one thing. I never want to let her go.

Monday mornings are always a chaotic mess, but at least Natalie is smiling again. Her girl's night with Chloe worked wonders on her psyche, and she now realizes that even though many men *are* jerks doesn't mean *all* of us fit that mold.

The concept that Chloe used me as the type of man to strive for blows my mind.

Actually, Chloe blows my mind—in all the right ways.

Once the girls leave for school, I head next door, eager to see the woman who gives me something to look forward to each day.

"Morning," I call out, smiling when Chloe pokes her head out of the kitchen. As per usual, she's got her glasses on and a bun on top of her head. She may be the antithesis of fashionable, but she's everything adorable in this world.

"Good morning. Did you eat?"

"No time this morning. Mia didn't want to get out of bed."

"Can you blame her? It's positively frigid. It took me twenty minutes to coax myself out of bed."

Yep, that did it. Mind? Straight to the gutter.

I can't help it. I've wanted to touch this woman for weeks. Any mention of her body and bed in the same sentence, and I don't stand a chance.

"What smells so good?" I ask, stopping short as I walk into the kitchen.

"I made you breakfast. I figured since you had the girls that you might be running behind."

There, on the table, is a spread that would make a diner weep. Eggs, bacon, sausage, pancakes, fruit, and juice are laid out, along with two place settings.

"This looks fantastic."

"Don't stand around and stare at it. Dig in."

She doesn't have to tell me twice. I'm starving, and I know she's a mean cook. It's a win-win. Glancing up, I smile when I notice Chloe is wearing the choker. "I was right. It looks stunning on you."

"I love it," she replies, fingering the gold filigree. "I never get presents."

Okay, time to dive in with both feet. God, give me strength. "You know how you told Natalie to wait for the right guy instead of settling for just *any* guy? You need to follow that advice."

Chloe nods, taking a bite of eggs. "I know, but it's hard for me to get close to people. I tend to hold everyone far away from my heart."

"You didn't do that with me."

A flush crawls up her cheeks. "You're special."

No, beautiful, *you're* special.

"Are you going out with Zeke again? I saw you two speaking at Enid's party. I was about to intervene when he stalked off."

I really want to wring Zeke's neck for the stunt he pulled on their date. He goes out with this incredible woman and tricks her into paying? Disgusting.

Chloe leans back in her chair, a curious expression on her face. I get it. I threw her with the Zeke question. But if she sticks with me, she'll see it makes perfect sense. "I wish you *had* intervened. He was dogged about a second date, but once was enough torture for this lifetime."

Whew, one issue is out of the way.

"Good. You deserve to be with someone who appreciates you."

"Thank you."

"I'm serious. A man who treats you with respect and care while still rocking your world when the lights go out. Or you can leave them on—your choice."

"Sounds perfect. If you find any men fitting that description who are interested in me, send them my way."

There's my opening. I lean across the table, grasping her fingers.

"Have dinner with me, Chloe. I'm going to stop pretending I don't want to get to know you better. Much, much better. I only hope you feel the same way. I know you don't date men with young kids—"

"I do."

"I thought you said you didn't."

"I don't."

My brow wrinkles at this wordplay. "You're confusing the hell out of me."

She laughs, waving her hands. "I don't date men with young kids—after the last time—but I do feel the same way."

"Does that mean you'll make an exception?"

"I would love for you to be the exception," she murmurs, those dark eyes luminous as they meet mine.

This time, I know that sexy smile is for me. There's no doubt.

"Get over here," I order, wrapping my arms around her when she snuggles onto my lap.

Do I want to carry her upstairs and have my way with her? Absolutely, but Chloe deserves first-class treatment, something that's been sorely lacking in her life thus far.

So, I settle for kissing the most delicious mouth I've ever known. As I pull Chloe flush against me, her breath hitching when my tongue melds with hers, I know I could be happy spending every day like this.

Best part? We haven't even had our first date yet.

But I have one hell of an idea.

CHAPTER 12
CHLOE

I've pulled every single item of clothing from my closet in a desperate bid to find something suitable to wear tonight.

It's my first date with Aidan, and even though we've been out together several times, this time, it's for real.

We aren't friends grabbing a drink or listening to music.

We're going on a date.

Something we both swore we couldn't do with the other person.

Love had other ideas, at least where I'm concerned. Now, I hope Aidan feels some semblance of the emotion, as well.

I think he does. He acts like it. Hell, he's spoiled me more than anyone else in my life, and we *weren't* dating at that point.

I finger the gold necklace, smiling at the feel of the cool metal around my neck. I wear it every day. Not only is it beautiful, but it makes me feel close to Aidan when he isn't around. I also think he loves the fact that I love it, which is a bonus.

My phone rings, and I bite back a grin. It's the man of the

hour, and I'm hoping he can shed some light on our plans for the evening and how the hell I should dress. "Hi, how's your day?"

"About to get way better. Will you be ready to go within the hour?"

"About that—"

"Don't tell me you're canceling."

I can't help it—I smile at the disappointment in his voice. Glad to know he's looking forward to our date, too. "You're not getting *that* lucky."

"I'm not getting lucky now? Damn."

"Let me rephrase. You might get lucky, but you're not getting rid of me. What should I wear tonight?" My guess is somewhat dressy, considering he took Barbara to a fancy restaurant.

"Casual is fine. Jeans and a sweatshirt work."

"Oh, okay." So much for the trendy steakhouse.

Immediately, I push that thought from my mind. Who am I to expect some fancy dinner? That's a terrible mentality. In fact, I argued with Aidan several times about paying for the date. I feel obligated since he's spent so much money on me already, but he insisted on setting everything up tonight.

Besides, it doesn't matter *where* we go. I'm with Aidan.

"We both know I can dress for comfort." I throw a glance at the pile of clothes on my bed, realizing I won't need any of them. Just as well. Comfort trumps heels any day.

"You know what? Bring an extra set of clothes, just in case you don't want to do what I have planned."

"Please tell me we aren't hunting. I can't shoot Bambi."

Aidan laughs, his gravelly voice rolling over me like honey. "Definitely not. But bring a change of clothes. Nothing fancy or extravagant. Laidback, like us."

"Not a problem."

Part of me now wonders if we'll be camping in the woods.

In the winter.

In several inches of snow.

"I'll see you in an hour, Chloe."

Disconnecting the call, I shove my dresses back into the closet, glimpsing my reflection in the mirror. Clad in leggings and a sweatshirt, it's my typical home gear, an outfit Aidan has seen me in countless times.

Yes, he told me to dress comfortably, but I refuse to dress *this* comfortably. It's still a date, and I want to look pretty for him.

Sixty minutes later, Aidan is on my doorstep, looking much like he does when he comes to work. Don't get me wrong, he's still sexy with his day-old stubble, flannel, and jeans, but I assumed he might dress up a bit more.

Apparently, he wasn't kidding about the whole casual concept.

"You look beautiful, Chloe," he states, taking my duffel bag from me.

I'm still casual in a sweater and jeans, but I dolled myself up a bit with some makeup and jewelry. Let's not forget the killer lingerie I picked up the day before.

That was coming with me regardless of whether we sleep in a hotel or an igloo.

"Thanks. You always look handsome."

He smirks, glancing at his outfit. "I didn't have any time to get ready. I can run and shave if you'd like."

Pressing my hand to his cheek, I shake my head, offering him a chaste kiss. "No, you're perfect as is."

He is, too, at least as far as I'm concerned.

Aidan helps me into his truck, and we head toward the highway… and away from town.

That's interesting.

"I have something to admit," Aidan says, drumming the steering wheel.

"What's that?"

"I originally planned to take you to dinner, but something came up, so I had to cancel it."

"Okay, no problem." Actually, it *might* be a problem at some point. I've barely eaten today. Between nerves and my deadline, I subsisted on coffee.

"A buddy of mine asked me to check on his place. It's out of the way, deep in the woods, but how could I say no?"

"Out of the way and deep in the woods? Are you taking me there to kill me?" I'm kidding—kind of.

Aidan laughs, shaking his head. "Wasn't planning on it. I figure we'll get there in about thirty minutes, and then I have a few repairs to take care of for him."

"Repairs?" My head spins with the onslaught of information.

"He's having some issues with his storm doors, and with the weather being what it is, he didn't want to wait. It won't take more than a couple of hours. Is that okay?"

I manage a nod. "Of course. I can help, or at least I can try."

Aidan skims his fingers along my jaw, sending me a smile. "I knew you'd be okay with it. Most women? They'd flip when they realized their date had turned into a work party. But not you."

Am I disappointed? Terribly, but he's helping his friend. Besides, most of my dates resemble the one I went on with Zeke —halfway decent food at a bar or chain restaurant, where nine times out of ten, I picked up the tab for us both.

This is different, and despite my hope for a romantic evening, we're together. Even if it's the wrong kind of screwing and hammering.

"I love that you're helping your friend. Can we stop at a fast-food place? I'm a little hungry, and I don't want to get a headache. I'll buy us something for while we work."

"No can do. There's nothing around here."

Staring at my lap, I suck in a deep breath, wishing I'd brought a package of crackers with me. "I'm sure there's water at your friend's house, and that should fill me up until we're finished."

He snaps his fingers, a smile breaking across his face. "Actually, that's a fantastic idea. I'll bet he has a few cans of food we can heat—beans or canned chili or something."

"Great." It sounds terrible, but I won't let Aidan know that fact.

Now at least I know why he told me to dress for comfort.

He turns up the radio, singing along to a John Mellencamp song, and I focus my gaze out the window, my insecurities backing up on me.

Maybe I heard Aidan wrong when he asked me out. Perhaps he never intended for it to be a *date* date.

That's likely it. I heard him wrong. Deep breath, Chloe. Suck it up and help him out. That's what friends do.

But despite my internal mantra, I'm on the verge of tears, which is silly, really. It's just dinner, not a funeral.

Forcing a smile, I pivot in my seat, determined to get this night back on track. "Maybe we can find a bar after we fix the storm door? I'll buy you a beer and burger."

"Like I said, there's not much up here. A can of beans will do me just fine. I actually ate before we left, so I'm not hungry, but I brought a six-pack of beer."

Aidan ate before we left? Didn't he invite me to dinner? Why wouldn't he tell me we would be nowhere in the vicinity of food?

That hunting idea is looking better and better. Bambi, I may be gunning for you before the night is over.

We pull down a long, dark road, and I hunker down in my seat. I'm used to the bright lights of Manhattan, but here in the mountains, it's pitch black.

Pitch black and surrounded by woods with all manner of creatures. Creatures with claws and teeth. Animals that may be willing to fight me for my can of beans.

"Are you scared?" Aidan shoots me a grin.

"I'm a big city girl in the middle of the woods. A bit out of my element."

"I'll protect you. It's right down here at the end of the road."

The truck crests the hill, and my eyes widen as we pull into the driveway of a gorgeous log cabin. The landscaping is fantastic, playing off the trees and tiered gardens, and even from here, I see at least two decks that undoubtedly have incredible views.

"Wow, this is beautiful."

"Nice, right?"

"Are the lights always on?" I ask, noticing the warm glow from the interior.

"Timer. He knew I was coming, so he turned them on."

"The wonders of the internet," I murmur, hopping out of the truck.

Aidan grabs our bags as he leads me to the front door. "It might be chilly inside, but I'll get a fire started."

"Can't be any worse than Betsey's house that first morning," I grin, stepping into the foyer.

Aidan reaches around me, flipping on another light. "I'm hoping it's a bit better."

When the light floods the room, my breath lodges in my chest. There are flowers everywhere—several bouquets and rose petals leading to a roaring fireplace. On the table is a bottle of champagne chilling in an ice bucket, along with several covered trays of food.

I spin around, my mouth slack with confusion. "I don't understand. Your friend did this?"

Aidan drops our bags, sliding his hands along my jaw. "My friend doesn't own this place. I rented it for the weekend. I know dinner is standard for a first date, and you deserve something spectacular. This is for us. It's also why I was running late. I had to get everything set up."

God, I love this man.

My heart wants to burst as I throw my arms around his neck, tears rolling down my face.

"I hope those are happy tears," Aidan states, running his thumbs along my cheeks.

"They are. No one has ever done anything like this for me."

"I wanted to make it memorable."

Pressing a kiss to his lips, I smile. "It's memorable because I'm with you."

"I'll give you credit, Chloe. You sure handled those curveballs well."

"I was wondering if I might have to hunt Bambi for food."

"I thought the canned beans were the tipping point."

"They were certainly the *low* point of the conversation." I walk into the living room, clapping my hands with glee. "This is incredible. All of this is ours?"

"For the entire weekend."

I grab a piece of fruit from one tray, popping it into Aidan's mouth. "Admit it. You're a romantic."

"I have my moments, but it has to be with the right woman."

"You have many." Suddenly, my hunger for food disappears, replaced by one far more ravenous. Grasping the edges of my sweater, I pull it over my head, hearing Aidan's breath hitch. "Can we hold off on dinner for a bit?"

He's at my side in a second, his fingers undoing the buttons on his shirt. "I'm so damn glad you said that."

The last month of feverish, caged emotions unlocks as we tear at each other's clothes, desperate to finally—*finally*—be together. Within seconds, we're naked, save for his boxers and my lingerie, and I can tell by the fire of desire burning in Aidan's eyes that he's equally close to the breaking point.

Aidan is far more beautiful under his clothes. I pause, drinking in the contours of his chest and shoulders, lightly dusted with hair and a happy trail leading to a cock that I know will make me *very* happy. I stroke my nails along his bulge, feeling his girth as his head drops back on a moan.

"What you do to me, Chloe," he murmurs, his eyes heady with lust.

He hasn't seen anything yet. Holding that emerald gaze, I slip my fingers beneath the waistband of his boxes, pulling them down as I drop to my knees.

Scratching my nails along his hair roughened thighs, I wrap my hands around his narrow hips, letting my tongue tease the tip of his cock. Aidan's low gasp only spurs me on as I glide my tongue along the underside of his shaft, one hand gently massaging his balls.

"Tell me what you want," I breathe, my voice a heated demand. "Show me exactly what you've been waiting for, and don't you dare hold back."

Aidan wraps his hand in my hair, his cock pulsing as he fucks my mouth. There's something about owning a man, knowing they're teetering on the brink of control, that drives me crazy. I feel Aidan's resistance wavering, his body trembling as I suck him deep, my tongue working his every inch.

"Fuck, Chloe, that feels so good."

But I know I can do even better, drive him past the point of madness to where all exquisite pleasure lies. Relaxing my throat, I take him all in, my fingers drifting along the crack of his ass to tease his rim.

That does it. Aidan bucks against me, low grunts escaping his lips as he demands everything my mouth will give him.

"Chloe, I need inside you."

There's no way I'm stopping now. Not until I feel him shatter before me. I keep coaxing him toward his own release, loving that no matter how he fights it, my tongue will win this battle. With a cry, he comes in a hot rush, growling through his orgasm.

After spending another minute providing post-release torture, I meet his gaze, licking my lips for effect. The truth is that the man is delicious.

He stumbles back, catching himself against the table as he catches his breath. "Holy fuck," he murmurs, running a hand through his hair as he fights to regain some semblance of control.

With a sexy smile, I pop a grape in my mouth, rising on tiptoe to tickle his lips. "Are you hungry now? Did that work up your appetite?"

"I'm ravenous… for you." Aidan takes back control as he grabs me about the waist, guiding my legs around him. He nuzzles my mouth, delivering tiny nips to my lower lip.

Without a word, he walks us to the bedroom, lowering us to the mattress. He slides his hand along my slick skin, so wet and desperate for his touch.

I writhe against him as he sinks his fingers inside me, his gaze focused on my face. "It's my turn, sweets. Do you know what this gorgeous body has done to me these last weeks? What you've done to me?"

"Show me," I manage, as Aidan flips me on top of him,

pulling my pussy to his waiting mouth. "Oh, yes," I moan, his hands banding around my thighs as his tongue wraps around my clit.

Aidan is tireless as he works me over, his tongue sinking deep inside me before returning to the delicious torture of my clit. I knot my hands in his short hair, earning a grunt of approval. My toes curl as I press my body ever closer to his mouth until pleasure rips through me, exploding across every cell.

I fall to the mattress, my breath coming in heated pants. Aidan climbs on top of me, his erection pressing deliciously against my stomach as our addiction to one another demands to be fed. Grabbing a condom from the bedside table, he tears it open and slides it down his length before plunging deep inside me.

I lock my legs around his waist, my hips meeting his every thrust. Then I slow him down, squeezing around him as his face contorts from the exquisite feeling. On and on, we play, bringing each other to the brink before backing down, only to repeat the torture all over again.

Suddenly, his hands wrap around my hips, arching them up as he pulls all the way out before plowing back inside me. He knows I'm right there, and he's determined to push me off that cliff.

With a scream, I grip the sheets, my entire body tingling with pleasure. Moments later, Aidan comes, a shout escaping his lips as he collapses on top of me.

"Well, you are just fabulous," I whisper, unable to wipe the smile from my face.

"Chloe, I can honestly say you are the best I've ever had, and I plan on several more helpings this weekend. Actually, I plan on several more helpings tonight."

THE MAN ISN'T KIDDING ABOUT BEING RAVENOUS, BUT I hardly mind. In between our sexual Olympics, we spend time hiking, cooking, and relaxing in the hot tub. I was right; the view is spectacular, and I don't mean the mountains.

Seeing Aidan by my side, that smile on his face before he kisses me, feeling his arms around me while we doze, are pleasures I never knew I'd experience in this life.

The truth is that Aidan has *brought* me to life. Now, I plan on returning the favor with the fiercest love I possess.

He's worth every ounce.

CHAPTER 13
AIDAN

,

I've had good sex before. Hell, I've had great sex. But there's something about being inside Chloe—every back-bending, toe-curling moment—that I can't get enough of.

Seriously.

Men think about sex pretty much all the time. An eighty-twenty split. With Chloe? It's ninety-nine percent of the time, and even that one percent involves her somehow.

The woman consumes me. She's fantastic. Everything I never knew I needed in my life. Not only is she the most talented lover ever, but she's also my best friend. Chloe has become inseparable from my girls, and I'm not sure who loves her more—them or me.

We spent the Christmas holiday together as one big, happy, extended family. Chloe is a master with buying presents. She's not one of those gift card queens. She puts a ton of thought into every gift, right down to the wrapping.

She shocked the hell out of me with a Martin guitar. I'd been eyeballing the beauty on our last few visits into town, but I never dreamed she would buy it for me.

Of course, my gift to her wasn't too shabby, either—brand new leather armchairs for her almost completed reading nook. They cost a pretty penny, but they'll look incredible next to the fireplace.

Then, just to make her smile, I sent her to the most expensive spa in the area. The woman never treats herself, so I made certain *I* did.

Now, it's well into January, but despite the winter chill, I'm always warm around Chloe. We've only been dating for a little over a month, but I feel ready to take our relationship to the next level.

I only hope she's on board with the idea.

"Can we talk?"

Chloe sucks in a slow deep breath as if readying herself for a deep conversation. "Yes. Actually, I need to speak with you, too."

This might be easier than I thought.

Stroking her hair, I press a kiss to her mouth. "It's not a bad talk. Promise."

"Okay. Go ahead."

I trace aimless patterns along her leg, the primal urges simmering just below the surface whenever she's close to me. "I love being with you. I've never had more fun in my life, but I'd like to be closer."

"Closer?" she smirks, glancing at our entangled bodies. "Don't know if that's possible. Are you trying to talk me out of my trip to New York?"

I hate that she's flying back north, but I get it. She has obligations and an apartment. Still, the idea of her being away from me for a week hurts like hell.

Here goes nothing. "What I mean is, I'd like to feel you when we're having sex. All of you. Have you ever thought of going on birth control?"

Chloe's eyes widen as she flops back against the cushions. "Shit. I can't."

"Is there a medical reason? That's fine if there is; I just wanted to take you raw, considering we aren't with anyone else."

I feel the trembles emanating from her body and wonder what news she's about to hit me with.

"Chloe? Please tell me you aren't seeing someone else." I don't honestly know how I'd deal with that bomb.

She chuckles and shakes her head before pivoting to face me. "Of course, I'm not seeing anyone else. I'm with you every day, remember?"

"I like you being with me every day. One might say I'm addicted to you." I steal another kiss from her gorgeous mouth, unsure what's going on in her head. "What did you have to talk about?"

"Umm... well..." Now she's stalling and, judging by her face, panicked over her disclosure.

Wonderful. Maybe she's tired of being with me every day and wants some space between us. Perhaps that's what the trip to New York is about.

"The thing is, Aidan... I'm not on birth control because I planned on having a baby, remember?"

The silence rings out after her statement, my mouth opening and closing like a fish gasping for breath. To be honest, I feel like I'm gasping for breath. "I'm sorry, what?"

"I thought you'd remember our conversation. Not long after I got here, we talked about how I wanted to have a child. How I was seeing a doctor in New York."

The balloon of happiness that is my life? Popped into a

million shards with the pin of her declaration. "Wait, a second. You're still considering having a baby?"

"I still want a baby." Her voice is quiet, unsure, and under normal circumstances, I would back off and simmer down.

Not happening. Not under *these* conditions.

"Why?" I bark, scrubbing my face with my hands.

"I'm not sure how I'm supposed to answer that question. For a million reasons, Aidan."

"I didn't know you were still considering it. You haven't mentioned it since that day. Is that why you're returning to New York? To be inseminated with some stranger's baby?" I feel my anger rising at the idea of her doing just that; returning to Asheville, pregnant with another man's baby and acting like we could just pick up where we left off.

Wouldn't that be the icing on the cake?

"I have an appointment with my doctor, but it's just a hormone levels check. I would never be inseminated without speaking to you."

"That's good of you."

She wrings her hands, the nervousness evident. "I know this is a big conversation, but I didn't want to wait any longer to discuss it. I'm not getting any younger, and I really want to have a child—which, you knew. Does it bother you that much to know I still want to have a baby?"

I jump to my feet, tugging a hand through my hair as I pace the rug. "Hell, yes, it bothers me, Chloe. I told you, I don't want any more children. I have three already."

"You never actually said you didn't want more children. You told me, you only dated single mothers." When my eyes widen, she raises her hands in surrender. "I understand your point of view."

"Obviously, you don't, because here we are, discussing the possibility of you having a baby."

"That's just it. We're discussing *me* having a baby. I never expected you to be involved. Do I want you to be? Of course, because you're an amazing man, but it's apparent you don't want any part of it. I still want to be a mother, though."

"Get a dog." I regret the words the moment I speak them, as she visibly winces under my verbal attack.

Chloe bites her lip, averting her gaze. "Now you sound like Charlie."

Great. I sound like her asshole ex. The one who chewed her up and spit her out. "I'm sorry for that comment. You didn't deserve that."

"Aidan, I'm not asking for anything beyond your understanding and acceptance."

"I understand your position. I do, but I can't be any part of this situation."

"This situation meaning us, as a couple?"

"Yes." I pray my stern stance will be enough to snap her out of this train of thought. We're perfect, as is. Why muck it up?

"Even if you have zero involvement in the child's life?"

My head is spinning after this conversation. I never saw this one coming. Chloe knew my position. Who does she think she is, changing the rules on me? "Even then. If you decide to have a baby, we're done."

Chloe sucks in a breath before standing and pulling on her coat. "I have to go."

When she turns to grab her bag, I see tears streaming down her face. Tears I caused her. Pain I caused her. "Shit. Don't cry, Chloe." I move to hug her, but she sidesteps me, maintaining a safe distance.

"It's fine. I mean, it isn't fine, but what did I expect? Thank you for your honesty, Aidan. Brutal, perhaps, but at least I know where I stand. Where we stand."

"Where is that?"

"Apparently, nowhere."

I huff out a sigh, perching on the arm of the chair. "I don't see why you need a child to complete you."

"And I don't see how you can't understand my desires, considering how much you love your girls."

"I adore them, but I don't want more kids."

She throws up her hands, her lips pursed in a thin line. "I heard you the first few times, Aidan. No need to keep repeating the joyous news. Besides, I didn't ask you to be the father, did I?"

Her temper is riled, as evidenced by the flashing in her dark eyes. Still, her words hit against me like fists. Why wouldn't she ask me? Why wouldn't I be her first choice? She wants a random sperm donor instead of me? I'm a damn good father. Even though I don't want more children, why doesn't she consider me a good enough choice for her baby?

"You act like I'm a monster for being upset, Chloe. You plan on having some random guy's kid, and I'm supposed to okay with that scenario?"

"No, I hoped you *wouldn't* want me to do that."

"I don't." Thank God we agree on something.

"I had hoped *you* would consider it. I know it isn't what you planned, but you aren't what I planned, either. That doesn't make it any less wonderful. I'm so happy with you and your girls, but I still have my dreams, too. I guess I thought we might make them happen together."

Christ, she's killing me right now. Her tear-stained face and the desperation in her voice, the soft urgency pulling at my heart to reconsider.

But I must stay the course. She knew my rules.

"I've had my family. If you pursue this, then…" I trail off, not wanting to breathe into life the possibility that Chloe and I are over. I just found her.

She pulls open the front door. "Goodbye, Aidan."

Then she's gone, eaten up by the night.

I sink into the couch, dropping my head in my hands. What the fuck just happened? Chloe and I were happy. Ridiculously happy. Then, out of nowhere, she drops this baby bomb in my lap. What did she expect me to say?

Did she think I would smile and tell her how excited I was at the prospect? That it didn't bother me that she planned to have another man's baby? Is she out of her mind?

I only hope that after sleeping on it, Chloe will return to her senses and realize what a ridiculous notion this baby idea is.

Then, we can go back to the way we were, never to discuss her being inseminated again.

I barely sleep that night, tossing and turning as visions of Chloe pregnant run rampant through my dreams. Her with a child, a child that isn't mine.

At six o'clock, I give up on the idea of sleep and drag myself to the coffeepot, no less angry at the woman for upending our stasis.

Who takes a perfect relationship and throws it away?

Chloe Strickland, obviously.

Glancing out the living room window, I notice the taxi parked in her driveway, ready to take her to the airport. A knot forms in my stomach when I catch sight of her, walking down the path, suitcase in hand.

"Chloe," I call, opening the front door.

When she turns in my direction, I'm struck by the pain rampant in her face. Not sure why she's so damn upset. She screwed up *my* life last night.

"Have a good trip." Hey, at least it's cordial.

"Thank you." Her voice is barely audible as she pauses, her hand on the back door of the cab. "Tell Mia happy birthday. I left her gift in the hall closet."

The woman adores my girls, and it's such genuine love. She never forgets a date or event. Hell, she's even bailed me out a couple of times. Suddenly, a bit of anger slides away as I realize there's no point in hating one another.

Besides, I don't think I could ever hate Chloe.

"I'm sorry."

She nods, her gaze focused on some distant point. "You told me your rules and have proven to be a man of your word. This is all my fault. We never should have gotten involved. We don't want the same things from life. I just thought"—she breaks off, the tears running down her face—"I thought love could fix everything. I've always been a very naïve woman. That much is apparent. Goodbye."

She slips into the cab, and it pulls away, leaving me to wonder how things got so off course.

I'M NO BETTER A FEW DAYS LATER, AND JUDGING BY the look on my ex-wife's face when she drops off the girls, I'm about to get it with both barrels.

Figures. Women always side together.

"What happened?" she asks, her nails drumming the counter.

"Should I play dumb and pretend I don't know what you're talking about?"

"I wouldn't advise it, Aidan. I want to know why you fucked up the greatest relationship you've ever had."

My jaw slackens at her accusation. "Me? It was all Chloe. All I did was tell her I don't want any more children—a fact *she* already knew. She's the one who threw the idea of having a baby at me. Talk about coming out of left field."

"You knew Chloe wanted a child. Besides, did she ask *you* to take on any of the responsibility?"

"No, she's planning on being inseminated with some stranger's kid."

"You'd be off the hook, then?"

I gape at my ex-wife. "She'd be a single mother, with no father around. If I'm dating her, I'll wind up in the paternal role."

"Is that what she stated or what you assumed?"

"It's obvious, Enid. How could I not?" Seriously, are all the women in my vicinity daft? This situation is black and white. Plain and simple.

"The way Chloe has taken on a maternal role for our daughters?"

Enid is not letting this topic drop, and with each question, I become more agitated. "That's different. They're already here."

"That is such a bullshit answer, Aidan."

I shrug, trying to throw off the weight of my decision. "I told Chloe if she was staying with me, then the baby idea was off the table."

"Please tell me you aren't this much of an asshole."

Now, I'm the asshole? That's rich. "I was clear from the beginning. I told her I respected whatever choice she made."

"You didn't give her a choice. You backed Chloe into a corner. She was given that option once before, and she chose his love over her desires. I doubt she will be that foolish again."

Her words enter territory I haven't wanted to consider—that Chloe might not return to Asheville. "You don't think she'll come back?"

"I sure as hell wouldn't if I were her."

"She's not you."

"You're right. She's put up with far more crap than I ever would. One last thing, and then I'll shut up."

I huff out a sigh before meeting her blue gaze. "What?"

"If it's the right decision—your decision to not have a child and pursue a future with Chloe—then why are you so damn miserable? Look at you. Have you slept since she left? You look like shit. If this is the right answer, why do you look like you've lost your best friend? Think about it."

"Enid," I call after her, waiting until she turns around. "Are you feeling any better? You look like you're losing weight."

I know it's a change of topic, but it's a legitimate question. I may look like shit, but Enid doesn't look much better. In fact, she seems progressively worse every day.

"Don't change the subject."

"Enid," I repeat, motioning to her. "I'm worried."

"They're running tests. It's probably early menopause. I'll keep you posted."

I recall Chloe mentioning that fact and realize she's only a couple of years younger.

No wonder she wants a baby. The clock is ticking.

Still doesn't change my stance on the situation.

Enid caves with a sigh, wrapping me in a hug before giving me a slight shake. "You're smarter than this. You know that, right?"

What neither woman seems to realize is I'm only sticking to my original plan. "I told her my position right from the beginning."

"Did you ever tell her you didn't want more children?"

"I'm sure I did." Although, as I rack my brain, I can't recall if I ever said those words.

"Did Chloe ever tell you she wanted a child?"

"Yes." The second I admit it, the heaviness returns to my chest. Chloe told me she wanted a baby. I assumed she changed her mind. Now, she's getting inseminated with some stranger's kid, and when she returns, I'll have to watch her grow round with someone else's baby.

If she returns.

Isn't that fucking wonderful?

"What would have happened if she got pregnant? Because I know you two couldn't keep your hands to yourselves."

"What do you mean?"

"Do I have to explain the birds and bees to you, Aidan?"

I scowl at Enid. "We would have had a baby."

"Would you have been mad? If you two had a whoops?"

"No." The moment I utter the word, I know it's true.

"Have you ever stopped to consider that perhaps it isn't Chloe having a baby that upsets you, but the idea she might have one with someone else? Here's a crazy concept—you could have a baby with the woman you love. Stranger things have happened." With a pat on my hand, she walks out the door, leaving me alone with my thoughts, which is *not* a safe place to be right now.

I ORDER PIZZA BECAUSE I HAVE NO DESIRE TO COOK. That, and Chloe had taken over the cooking, which I was more than happy to allow. She's a far better chef, even convincing Mia to try green beans.

Talk about a win.

As I clean up the counter, a picture Emily drew falls out. It's of the family, complete with a tiny brunette. Chloe. I trace my finger over the image, that tightness in my chest returning.

I miss her. Way more than I'm willing to admit.

"You're an idiot."

Turning, I offer my eldest daughter a glare. "Excuse me?"

"She was great for you. For all of us."

"She wanted different things from life."

"No, she didn't. She just wanted to have a baby. You know, Chloe was willing to take on all of this, no questions asked. Your kids, your life. Why couldn't you be willing to give her what she wants? Isn't that what relationships are about?"

Natalie's words damn near bring me to my knees. "When did you get so damn smart?"

"My daddy didn't raise no fool. You love kids, Dad. What's the big deal?"

She's not lying. I've always adored kids and loved the idea of a noisy house full of laughter and the all too occasional tantrum. Hey, you have to take the bad with the good.

"But you guys are older. You want a baby running around the house?"

Natalie shrugs. "If it would make you guys happy, sure. Besides, I'm leaving for college soon. I'll have to see it for cute shit and holidays."

Usually, I would mention her cursing, but she's right. Everything she says is accurate, even if my stubborn ass won't admit it. "You're a ton of help."

"Maybe you'll finally have your son. Think about it, Dad. You were happy. I never remember seeing you happy like that before, and now, you're miserable."

She walks away, but the heaviness remains. Seems no matter what I do, I can't shake this lost feeling since Chloe left my life.

CHAPTER 14
CHLOE

New York is in the middle of its coldest winter in years, but I barely feel the frigid air on my face as I exit my apartment building onto the bustling street.

As always, Manhattan is a hubbub of activity, but for the first time, I'm overwhelmed by all the people. I finally understand how my mother felt when she desired an escape from all the noise.

I miss the mountains of North Carolina, the overly nosy neighbors, the fresh air. Mostly, I miss Aidan, even though I know we're a lost cause.

He made his stance very clear before I left, and I feel foolish for even broaching the topic. Enid and I discussed me telling him about my desire to have a baby, and she swore he would be open to the idea.

But he wasn't.

His opinions sliced through me, making me question every decision.

Making me question the idea of having a child.

Everyone says being a single mother is tough, but I thought I could handle it. I was so foolish to think, for one second, that Aidan might be on board with having a baby together.

It played out so differently in my head. There, he was surprised but happy. Eager even to have this little life the two of us created.

In reality, he mocked me, asking why I couldn't get a dog and be happy with my lot in life. In that way, he was much like Charlie, who always wondered why I wanted anything beyond what crumbs he offered.

Imagine if I broached the idea of marriage *and* a baby? Aidan would have melted down right in front of me.

One thing is for certain. I've learned my lesson. No man wants to have a family with me, so if I want a baby, my only option is with a stranger's sperm. Funny, it was such a normal concept only a few months ago, but now it feels like cheating on Aidan.

Not that it matters. We're done.

I walk into my doctor's building, riding the elevator to the eleventh floor. As usual, the waiting room is packed, but by some miracle, I'm called within a few minutes.

My doctor is a sweet man with seven children of his own. That's right. Seven. He had six with his first wife, but she died in a car accident. A few years later, he met another woman and fell in love. But she desperately wanted a baby. His reply? He was overjoyed to have a baby with her, thrilled to have that chance to make her happy.

I wish I could meet a man like that, but at this point, there *is* no point, and certainly no man.

"How have you been, Chloe? I'm sorry about your mother. Your file says that's why you canceled our last appointment." He smiles at me. "I thought perhaps you'd met a nice man and fallen in love."

His sentiment brings a fresh onslaught of tears, but I blink them back. I will *not* fall apart in my doctor's office.

"No man, just dealing with my mother's estate." Why go into specifics? There is no man, at least not anymore.

He perches on the stool, studying me. "You told me last time that you would be ready to proceed this winter. Are we still on the same path?"

"I… I…" the words stick in my throat as I struggle to form a sentence.

The doctor pats my knee, his smile fading as the tears spill down my cheeks. "What is it, dear?"

"I can't do this." Dashing out the door, I run out of the building and onto the street, barely missing several patches of ice.

Leaning against a storefront, I sob, the tears and snot mixing in a mess of emotions. "Damn him."

Not only does Aidan not want me or a child with me, but he's also made me doubt my ability to do it on my own. I know it's not his fault. It's not like he stopped me from leaving. I could go back to the doctor right now and be inseminated within the week.

That's not the problem.

I fell in love. I want a baby with the man I love. A baby with big green eyes and dimples like his dad.

But Aidan doesn't want that, at least not with me, and it doesn't matter what I want.

I don't get a say.

Dragging my sleeve across my face, I huff out a breath. Time to get it the fuck together. This isn't the first time a man has knocked me on my ass, but I know one thing—it *will* be the last time.

There's a great coffee shop near the doctor's office, so I head into the decadent warmth and order a large latte. Then I slide into an empty booth and pull out my phone, emailing my realtor.

My new plan? Sell Betsey's house as soon as possible and use the monies to buy a small home upstate. Then, I'll get a damn dog and probably several cats to round out my childless collection.

The coffee warms my bones, but there's nothing hot enough on this planet to thaw my heart.

Maybe I can live without that organ.

"Chloe, is that you?"

Looking up, my heart catches. Standing there, not three feet from me, are the boys I raised for five years. Henry and Jeff, their father right behind them.

"Look at you two. You've gotten so big."

The boys dash over to me, engulfing me in a hug, their excitement evident.

"We missed you so much, Chloe."

"I never thought we would see you again."

You weren't supposed to, boys.

Jeff, the more sensitive of the two, wipes away a tear on my cheek. "Are you sad, Chloe?"

His sweet heart always knew how I was feeling. It's nice to know some things don't change.

"No, I'm just sniffling from the cold. It's freezing out there. How are you two?" I nod toward Charlie, hovering near the table and watching the scene play out with a great deal of interest. "Hi, Charlie."

"Mind if we join you?" he asks, and I motion to the empty seats.

In a crazy turn of events, I spend the next thirty minutes with the man and boys I dedicated five years of my life to before Charlie whisked them away to a new one. Henry and Jeff are handsome, intelligent, and well-mannered.

I'd like to think I had something to do with that.

Charlie and his wife are divorcing—again. To hear him tell it, it was hell, almost from the beginning. I feel for them all. It's hard when families fall apart.

"Would you like to have dinner?" Charlie asks, a hesitant smile on his mouth. "The boys really miss you. We all miss you."

No matter how handsome Charlie is, I won't tread that road again. He broke me once, but Aidan broke me worse.

I'll never let another man break me again.

The rest of my life is going to focus on me… and my clowder of cats.

I wrap an arm around each boy, squeezing them tight. "Thanks for the offer, but I have to fly back to North Carolina."

Is it the truth? Not exactly, although I will have to go back there at some point. However, it's an easy way to get out of dinner without hurting Jeff and Henry. Charlie's heart, I'm not worried about.

"You don't live here anymore?" Henry asks.

"Right now, I live in both places, but I'm selling the North Carolina house."

"You don't like it down there?"

What is about children, asking the questions that rip apart the bandages holding your wounded heart together?

"I like it, but I don't fit in down there." I don't divulge falling in love with a man who wouldn't love me enough.

"Can we write you letters?" Jeff inquires, grasping my hand.

I glance at Charlie, who nods his approval, before giving the boys my address. "This is my North Carolina address. Since I have to fly down there for a bit, I'm having my mail forwarded. I'd love to get letters from you both."

Do I think I will? No, which is part of why I gave them the North Carolina address. I won't be there to see their letters not arrive.

With a few last hugs, I watch them leave, realizing it's likely the last time I'll ever see them. No doubt my address will conveniently disappear. I can't blame Charlie. It's too complex a situation, and I'm not their mother.

I'm not their anything.

Not anymore.

That idea brings on a new rash of tears, so I head for home, desperate for the familiar. But my tiny apartment is suffocating, and the noise overwhelming.

I slide on headphones to deaden the sounds of the street, wishing they made something similar to dull the pain in my heart.

No such luck.

My realtor calls from North Carolina. Maybe I already have a buyer. Wouldn't that be a trip?

Nope, no buyer, but a blizzard, heading for the area. She wants to know if I properly winterized my house, and with a start, I realize I haven't.

I can call Aidan or Enid, but I'd rather chew nails.

I can risk it, hoping the house will limp through unscathed, but a burst pipe will cost thousands in repairs and delay any potential sale.

With a sigh, I head for my closet.

Looks like I'm North Carolina bound.

CHAPTER 15

AIDAN

"Oh, Lord, please tell me the beard isn't making a comeback."

So much for getting any peace this morning.

Squinting up into the sun, I nod at the shadowy outline of my ex-wife. "Don't lie. I know you secretly miss the beard."

"I hate the damn thing." She pulls up a deck chair, huffing out a sigh as she sits. "Have you heard from Chloe?"

I shake my head, intent on repairing the broken lock in my hands. Seems I've found a myriad of projects to keep me busy these last few weeks, as the sinking sensation sets in that the woman I love isn't returning to North Carolina.

The first week was bad but tolerable. The second week was awful, and this week is pure unadulterated hell. The empty house next door looms as a reminder of what I let go of.

What I've lost.

"I blame myself for this situation. You know, I gave you way too much credit."

I shrug as I continue working. "I won't pretend I know to what you're referring. I'm not playing this game with you, Enid."

"I told Chloe to discuss having a baby with you. Pushed her to broach the subject."

"It was you?"

"I knew how important it was to her, and I mistakenly thought she was important to you."

"What the fuck is that supposed to mean?" My anger has ridden a razor's edge these last few weeks, and once again, it flies back into the red.

"She was terrified to discuss having a baby, but I was convinced she meant something to you after seeing you two together. God knows she made you happy. I assumed you might be open to returning the favor."

"She knew I didn't plan on more children. She knew my rules."

"You and your fucking rules, Aidan. Your rules didn't plan on a woman like Chloe."

Truer words were never spoken.

"I'm supposed to be fine with the fact she's having some random man's baby? Well, I'm not. I can't handle that concept."

"You idiot. You're not upset about the idea of a baby. You're upset that it wasn't going to be with you."

"That's not what I'm saying."

Enid sits forward, grasping my arm. "Yes, it is. It's written all over your face. Chloe wants a baby with *you*, Aidan."

"What makes you so sure?" And why does my heart skip a beat at the idea?

"She told me." Enid leans back with a slight groan. "Chloe knew your rules, but that didn't stop her from falling in love and wanting a baby with the man she loves."

Chloe never told me she loved me. She showed me in a myriad of ways, but we never spoke the words.

It hurts that Enid heard her say them aloud, but I never have. Now, I probably never will.

"Hmm." It's a bullshit response, but all I can manage right now, as I turn my attention back to the lock.

"She's a terrific mother to our girls. They need her in their lives."

"They already have a mother."

"That's what I need to speak to you about."

The words hang in the air, a sudden chill descending over me. "Enid, what the hell does that mean?"

"It means… I'm sick." Her eyes, those bright blue eyes, are glassy with unshed tears.

Jeff moves to stand next to Enid, his expression grim.

Suddenly, it's all so clear. Enid's exhaustion, weight loss, and pallor. Somewhere, deep in the dark recesses of my brain, I knew she was sick, but I couldn't let my heart accept that fact.

Blinking back tears, I look skyward. "How bad?"

"Fucking stage four pancreatic cancer. You know me. Go big or go home."

Despite my ex-wife's sad attempt at levity, there's no humor to be found here. A huge part of my heart shatters with the realization that Enid's lifeline will be cut drastically short.

I switch into action mode, hopping to my feet and pacing the deck. "Time to fight. What do we need to do? How are we kicking cancer's ass?"

Enid grasps my arm, giving it a squeeze. "We aren't, my love. They've given me a year."

You think you'll know how to react when you receive bad news as an adult. With enough years under your belt, you've heard it all. Seen it all.

What an utter crock of shit.

There is bad news, and then there is the *worst* kind of news.

Enid's diagnosis? *Way* past the worst kind.

With a strangled groan, I sink into the chair, rocking back and forth as I bury my head in my hands.

A year. One lousy year is all the time we have left with Enid? That's not possible.

I won't accept that truth.

"Let's get a second opinion."

"We have," Jeff states, stepping forward to wrap his arms around Enid.

"A third, then. A fourth. Hell, get a dozen opinions." With each word, my voice increases in volume. Perhaps if I yell loud enough, God might hear me.

"Aidan, we've gotten the opinions. They all suck." Enid wipes away a few tears, reaching out to grasp my hand.

"Shit, Enid. This doesn't work without you." And then I engulf them both in an embrace because I don't know what else to do. What else to say.

There's no way to accept the woman I've spent most of my life loving is dying. Our daughters are six, eleven, and sixteen. They need their mom for everything.

I can't wrap my head around the idea that Enid won't be there for their weddings, the birth of their children, their graduations, for God's sake.

I frame her face with my hands, gazing into the blue eyes I know so well. "What do you want to tell the girls?"

"The truth. I don't want to keep this from them. Our girls are too smart for that nonsense, and besides, each day now is a gift. I was hoping we could tell them today and then do something as a family. Ice skating, maybe. I want to continue to have fun until I can't anymore." She chokes out the last part, overcome by tears.

With a resigned sigh, I nod and try to make myself look presentable before I walk into the house, Enid and Jeff at my heels.

Enid is right. Our girls are far too intelligent. Natalie takes one look at our reddened eyes and starts shaking her head, the sobs already escaping her throat.

Poor Mia has no idea what's going on, but Emily senses the energy, walking over and grasping her mother's hands while offering a somber smile.

It's the worst moment of my life, watching the agony cross over my daughters' faces as we tell them about their mother's diagnosis. Never in my life have I felt so helpless. As a parent, you strive to protect your kids from every hurt in this world, but there's no protecting them from this.

And the girls are a mixed bag of emotions, ranging from anger to belligerence to denial—all in the space of a few moments.

Can't say I blame them. I feel the same way.

After explaining the severity of Enid's illness, Natalie dashes upstairs, slamming her door.

I wish Chloe was here.

The thought hits fast, remembering how she lovingly coaxed my daughter out of her room, making her smile when her heart was broken over a boy.

This time, Natalie's heart really *is* broken, and she needs Chloe's gentle love more than ever.

We all do.

But Chloe is gone. I made sure of it. I sent away the woman I love because she wanted a baby with me. She loved me enough to want a baby with me, and I shot her down, even throwing in a few insults for good measure.

Now, the one woman who could help hold this ragtag pack

together is hundreds of miles away, and I don't know what I could say to convince her to give me another chance.

My family needs her.

I need her.

I don't think I can do this without her, and I sure as hell don't want to try.

Enid spends a half-hour upstairs with Natalie before they both walk downstairs, eyes red and skin blotchy.

"We are going to have fun. Do you hear me?" Enid states, her voice surprisingly forceful. "That is enough tears for one day. I want laughter for the rest of it."

On that note, we head to the ice rink, determined to do Enid's bidding.

Do you know the hardest thing in the world is pretending to smile when your soul is shattered? Funny thing, though—the more you pretend, the more genuine the happiness becomes.

That's the thing with love. It's there through it all, holding us fast when without it, we would fall apart.

Still, I fear the quiet moments when the dark thoughts creep in, and there isn't enough noise to drown out their screams. My family will have many dark moments, but I must pray we'll have enough love to soldier on.

"I think that went well. Granted, I've never had to tell my family that I was going to croak before, but overall, stellar performance." Enid falls into place next to me, shooting me a grin.

"You and your macabre sense of humor. Not funny, Enid."

"You know, I may be dying, but I'm not dying today."

Grasping her hand, I press a kiss to her fingers. "I love you. You know that, right?"

"I love you, too. Do I get to make requests now, Make a Wish style?"

"What do you want? I'll make it happen."

She slows, pulling me to a stop. "Make things right with Chloe. I miss my friend. I miss the smile you wore whenever she was near you. You love her, and she loves you. Get married and have a couple of kids because you two will have gorgeous children."

Despite it all, I chuckle, even managing a nod. "They'd be adorable, but can you imagine the stubbornness? Chloe is the most stubborn woman I know, and our kids would be beyond in that department."

Enid's smile widens, and I realize I just described the children I swore I didn't want. "They'd be stubborn, wickedly smart, and funny, just like both of you. Pieces of your love that will live on long after you're gone. None of us know when this ride will end, Aidan. Do you really want to go through this world without Chloe, simply because of your rules?"

Blinking back tears for the millionth time today, I shake my head.

But what if it's too late? What if she never returns or, worse, returns with a baby in her belly? A baby that isn't mine.

It's too much to fathom with the myriad of emotions bouncing around my heart and head.

All I can do right now is try to hold my family together and pray for a miracle.

CHAPTER 16
CHLOE

The taxi drops me in front of Betsey's house at nine in the morning, and I hand the driver some cash before exiting the vehicle. Burrowing my face into the scarf, I suck in a deep breath, feeling wholly uncertain about being here again.

I steal a glance next door, thankful no one is stirring yet. I'm not ready to see them. Hell, I may *never* be ready to see Aidan.

I wonder if he's cozy with Barbara now. It has been three weeks. Our relationship is old news at this point.

With a sigh, I trudge up the walk, noting the steps are freshly cleared. My heart catches at the knowledge that Aidan has been keeping the walkways clean in my absence, but I shake off the emotion.

I can't allow myself to feel anything but contempt for the man who tore my heart apart.

Now, if I can just winterize the house and set up the listing with the local realtor, I can be on my way back north, never to see Aidan again.

One day, I'm sure I'll be okay with that decision.

***

I JERK AWAKE ON THE COUCH, REALIZING THAT MY lack of sleep these past few weeks has finally caught up. I only meant to rest my eyes. My eyes had other ideas. The house is also downright frigid, likely because I didn't bother to light the stove when I walked in, but that isn't what woke me.

From the back end of the house, I hear rustling, and my breath catches.

My biggest fear when I returned to Manhattan was that someone had burglarized my apartment in my absence. It happens—a lot. They watch your home, and they know when you're gone, especially when it's more than a week.

Especially when you live alone.

But my apartment was safe and sound. It seems the North Carolina house is the chosen victim.

Glancing around the room, I grab a heavy candlestick. I'm aware it won't do a damn thing against a gun, but I'll go down fighting.

False bravado, perhaps, but I need all the help I can get right now.

My mobile phone is upstairs, along with the rest of my stuff. As for Betsey's landline? In prime working order, not that there's a phone in this room.

Tiptoeing toward the back room, I heft the candlestick in both hands, prepared to swing this sucker like a baseball bat. I see someone digging through the closet as my heart threatens to pound out of my chest.

I do *not* want to die like this.

"What are you doing in my house?" I bellow, raising the candlestick over my head.

"What the hell? Chloe? You scared the shit out of me." The familiar voice rushes headlong into my brain, and I lower the candlestick as Aidan turns, those green eyes wide. "When did you get back?"

"Earlier today." Now that I know I'm not about to die, my entire body shakes from the adrenaline rush.

His gaze drops to the candlestick, the corners of his mouth quirking under his once-again bearded face. "What were you going to do with that?"

"Kill you. Possibly maim you. That was the original plan."

"And now?"

"Still viable options." As my breathing normalizes, a surge of anger flows through me as I look at the man I love.

The man who doesn't want me unless I throw away my life-long dream. The man who wouldn't even hear me out about wanting a child together.

"What are you doing here?"

He motions to the closet. "I was looking for my drill. Have to repair a neighbor's window."

Realizing it's a valid reason, I relent, holding up my hand. "Have at it." I turn toward the kitchen, the need for coffee growing by the second.

My coffee addiction is even worse now, likely because I substituted it for food most days.

"How are you?"

"Fine." It's a standard reply, one you give to the mail lady or a neighbor you hardly know. Not the answer you give to the man you wanted to spend your life with, the man you hoped would father your child. But it's all I can manage at the moment. "How are you?"

He follows me to the kitchen, leaning against the doorframe. "It's been a fucking terrible few weeks."

Turning on my heel, I catch the brightness in his eyes. Could he be referring to our breakup? Could it be bothering him one iota as much as it's bothering me? Is that possible?

Best to err on the side of caution. Likely has nothing to do with us. "I'm sorry to hear that."

"Are you pregnant?"

The coffee mug slips from my hands, and I thank God it's empty. "What?"

Snatching his ball cap off his head, he wrings it between his hands. "You had a doctor's appointment, right? You were only supposed to be gone a week, but it's been three weeks. I figured you had gotten… inseminated."

Tonging my upper lip, I contemplate lying to the bastard, telling him I'm happily knocked up, and he can just fuck all the way off. Sadly, it's not my style, although I would love to see his face when he heard the news.

It would likely relieve him, knowing he was off the hook.

Picking up the mug, I pour some coffee, not bothering to offer him any. "Not that it's any of your business, but I've decided against having a child."

I expect a smirk or a blank expression, but his brow furrows at my declaration. "Why?"

Did this blowhard just ask me why?

Slamming down the mug, I ignore the burn as droplets of coffee land on my skin. "Let's see. The men I've dated all thought me becoming a mother was the worst idea in the world, and considering they have children, they must be experts, right? You and Charlie obviously know something I don't. No surprise, really, that there's something wrong with me. My own mother didn't want me, so I'll just get a damn dog and forget the whole thing."

I surprise even myself with the anger spewing from my mouth. Is it deserved? Every last syllable.

"Please don't think like that, Chloe. I hate hearing you say those things." His eyes are bright, a muscle jumping in his jaw as he speaks the words.

"Why? I figured you'd be relieved, not that I planned on bothering *you* for anything ever again."

"You'll be an amazing mother. You are a natural nurturer; you make it look effortless. The way you are with the girls is incredible. Don't give up your dream, certainly not for stupid, misguided men."

I blink back tears, my strong front cracking with each nice word dripping from his hypocritical mouth. I need him gone and fast. "Doesn't matter. I'm fine with my decision. Anyway, did you get what you needed? I have a busy day with the realtor."

"You're selling?"

"Yep."

Aidan steps toward me, but I jump back, my back hitting against the counter.

He stops, his gaze falling to the floor. "I missed you."

A scoff flies from my mouth. "What am I supposed to say to that?"

"Maybe that you missed me, too?"

"What's the point? Let you close so you can hurt me again? No, thanks. I'm done being a glutton for punishment." I motion to his bearded jaw. "Barbara must be thrilled that her lumberjack is back."

Yes, it's a petty and unnecessary barb, but I'm not in the mood to take the high road. He deserves at least one jab.

"This," he rubs his hand over his jaw, "is laziness. I didn't know you were back, or I would have shaved. Also, I'm not with Barbara. I was with you. Just you."

"Emphasis on was."

"Chloe—"

The sound of his daughters entering the house interrupts our uncomfortable reunion. Some things never change, and I'm sure not holding them accountable for their father being an asshole.

The three of them race to my side and wrap their arms around me, exclaiming how much they missed me.

I missed them, too. In the last few months, they've become an integral part of my life—one that will now be relegated to my past.

"We miss you. When can we stay over?" Natalie asks, looping her arm through mine and laying her head on my shoulder.

"Soon. I have to get a few things organized, but then we'll have a girl's night. Sound good?"

"Our mom is dying," Emily states, her affect so flat I can't tell if she's joking. One look at Aidan solidifies the truth.

"What?" It's all I can manage as a feeling of desolation washes over me. "What do you mean?"

Aidan bites his lip, that brightness back in his eyes. "Stage four pancreatic cancer. She found out last week."

I struggle to stay upright at the news. Adults are supposed to be strong, particularly in the face of children. That's what we do, right? But I adore Enid, and the idea that she's dying, compounded with everything else, breaks me.

Her poor children. Her poor husband.

Poor Aidan.

"I hate this news so much," I exclaim, my cheeks wet with tears as I grip the girls to me. Squatting down, I force a smile, wiping my face. "You know what? We're going to have the biggest girl's night ever—you three, your mom, and me. I'll buy a ton of food, even more chocolate, and enough face masks for everyone. Then we'll play board games and watch silly movies all night. Okay?"

I realize one night of laughter won't cure what ails them, but I want to help provide as many happy memories as possible. There will be a plethora of sad ones in the future.

A car horn beeps outside, and the girls give me a final hug before tearing out the door, leaving Aidan and me staring at one other.

Running my sleeve under my nose, I force a grin and a sad shrug before crossing the room and burying my head in his chest. "I'm so sorry. My heart breaks for all of you. Let me know how I can help."

Life is funny. You think your problems are insurmountable until life shows you ones that truly are, making yours minuscule in the process.

Aidan wraps his arms around me, holding me close as he presses his lips to my hair. "I'm glad you're back."

Resting my chin on his chest, I shoot him a smile, but it's full of heartbreak. Right now, it's the best I can manage. "I'll help however you need—watching the girls or running errands."

Aidan grazes his hand along my cheek, his gaze soft. "That's not what I meant. I'm glad *you're* back. I missed you."

I missed him too, to the point of agony, but I can't walk that path again, no matter how much my heart wants me to.

"I'm going to say hello to Enid." It's a good segue, allowing me to step from the warmth of his embrace and put much-needed space between us. It also allows me to hug my friend, all while hopefully holding it together.

Enid hops out of her car, shaking her head, a rueful expression on her face. "I guess you heard the news. A banner year, isn't it?"

Pulling her to me, I squeeze my arms around her, willing the cancer away from the sheer force of my love. If only it were that easy. "I'm trying not to cry, but I suck at that."

Enid grins at me, an honest to God, genuine smile this time. "Yeah, you do. You know what? I need a drink, and I want to go somewhere they won't shoot my sympathetic looks. I'll have Aidan watch the girls a few hours more, and we will have some fun. That is if you'll come with me?"

I glance down at my usual attire—leggings and a sweatshirt. "Give me ten minutes."

Dashing into the house past Aidan, I grasp his arm. "Enid and I are going for a drink. We'll be back later."

"Okay. Be safe."

"I'll try not to dance on too many tabletops."

I'm halfway up the stairs when Aidan calls my name.

Looking back at him, I pause, wondering what else he has to say. Wondering if there *is* anything else to say.

He runs a hand over his beard, and for the first time, I see him struggling for the words. "Think about what I said." Without another glance, he spins on his heel, walking out the front door.

Now, what the hell does that mean? Aidan has said a lot of things, and lately, none of them good.

With a sigh, I climb the stairs. Time to focus on my friend, some drinks, and a few laughs.

ONE DRINK TURNED INTO THREE, ALONG WITH A dinner feast. We went to the trendiest restaurant in Asheville and blew obscene amounts of money.

But we laughed. We cried. We experienced every emotion in between.

Per Enid, it's terrible for people to know you're dying. Not because you hate them knowing, but it's like suddenly, you're made of glass, and everyone is waiting for you to break. She joked how people she knew couldn't stand her were now dropping off casseroles, and while she appreciated the gesture, the irony wasn't lost on her.

That's why she needed a night out with me. I might be sad and sappy, but at least it's genuine. She knows I loved her before she was handed her sentence.

She drops me off at a little past ten, and I walk into the house, smiling as I recall how we bopped in the car the whole drive back, singing our hearts out to eighties music.

Despite it all, the heartache and the unimaginable hole losing Enid will leave, we still laughed, and we meant every chuckle.

Rolling my shoulders, I pad into the kitchen, pulling out a glass of wine. Sue me, but I'm not entirely done for the evening. Then I flip on the radio and settle into one of the armchairs Aidan bought me for Christmas. They are truly amazing pieces of furniture, fitting perfectly into the reading nook that's ninety percent finished.

"Can I join you?"

I glance over my shoulder. There, with a freshly shaven face, is Aidan, wine bottle in hand. "Sure."

He pours himself a glass before walking into the nook, his eyes dancing over the shelves he constructed. "It's coming together."

"You do amazing work. It's hard to believe you're self-taught. You're a true artisan."

"A person can do anything they put their mind to, but you already know that. Hop up."

"Why?"

"Just hop up."

With a grunt, I stand, an exasperated scoff flying from my mouth when he sinks into my recently vacated chair. "Are you serious?"

Sending me that sexy emerald stare I know and love, Aidan takes my wine glass and sets it on the table before pulling me onto his lap. I should fight him on this, but I've had a few cocktails, and my defenses are down.

Besides, inside his embrace is my favorite place in the world.

Even if I'm still really, *really* angry with the man.

His hands glide along my thigh, inching me closer to his chest. "Enid said you two had a good time."

"We did. She had two rules. Couldn't use the 'c' word and had to be served by the hottest guy in the place."

"How'd that work out for you?"

With a sexy smirk, I pull a piece of paper from my pocket. "I got his number."

Aidan's eyes widen. "What the hell do you mean?"

"Our server gave me his number."

"What are you going to do with it?"

I shrug because, honestly, I hadn't thought that far ahead. "Call him, maybe? Crazy idea, I know."

"Give me that." Aidan rips the piece of paper into tiny bits before tossing them into the fire. "You're not calling him."

I stare at the flames as they destroy any evidence of the server's digits. "Did you seriously just rip up the hot guy's number?"

"You're not going to be with him, even if it sounds like a good idea. It isn't. It's actually a terrible idea. The worst."

My glare swings to his handsome face. He is *not* taking this stance. "Really? What's a good idea, then? Being alone?"

"Being with me, being with my girls."

Gripping the chair arm, I squirm in his arms. I need to escape—now. "You're the one who pushed me away, remember? No, I can't discuss this. *We* can't discuss—"

Aidan's lips capture mine, ending any argument as he sweeps me into a blistering kiss. He holds nothing back as his mouth claims mine, our tongues slicking together, growing more brazen by the second.

A low groan rises from Aidan's chest as his fingers knit in my hair. I've known, since our first kiss, how talented Aidan is with his mouth, but I've never felt him so desperate before.

Such intensive longing in every breath.

It's too much for my heart to handle, and my body has already surrendered.

When I try to pull back, he tightens his grip on my hair, deepening the kiss until all I feel is him and his hunger surrounding me.

Aidan stands with me still in his arms, his lips fused to mine.

He finally grants me some breathing room as he walks us through the house. "Where are we going?"

"Upstairs."

That single word reverberates through my lust-filled haze.

Planting my hands on his chest, I shake my head. Trust me, I *want* to have sex with Aidan. I've got a pleasant buzz going, and this man plays my body like the finest instrument. His mouth and hands should be gilded—they're that good—and don't even get me started on his cock.

But that's not the point.

He broke my heart, and a quick romp is *not* the way to fix this problem.

"Besides the messy emotional state of our lives, we can't have sex."

"Why?"

Let's try logic. Maybe that will work. "I don't have any condoms here. Do you have some?"

Aidan shakes his head, but he hasn't stopped moving toward the stairs.

"Where are we going?" I repeat.

"I told you. Upstairs."

"And I told you we don't have—"

"We don't need one." His green eyes spark as they hold my gaze, the desire raging in their depths.

"Did you get a vasectomy while I was gone?" Considering his current behavior and desire to throw caution to the wind, it's a distinct possibility.

"Of course not."

My eyes widen as I struggle to appear unaffected by his demands. "It's not a safe time of the month."

More logic, which apparently, Aidan has no qualm with throwing out the window.

A slow smile breaks across his magical mouth as he dusts kisses along my jaw. "Do you have any more obstacles you'd like to throw out there, or can I take you to the bedroom now and make love to you all night?"

Words I would have given anything to hear a few weeks earlier are now a mocking reminder of how we ended things before I left for New York.

"What are you doing, Aidan?" The false bravado has long since fled, leaving only uncertainty in its wake.

"Showing you that what you want, I want it, too."

"But you don't, remember? You made that very clear."

"I was wrong."

My rational brain bursts into the moment, overruling any

further chance of playtime. I know what he's doing and why he's doing it.

I can't allow it.

It isn't fair, especially not to me.

"Please, put me down. Aidan, I know you're hurting, and you feel lost with everything happening with Enid, but that's not a reason to say these things. Certainly not a reason to claim to want me and want what I want."

Part of me expects Aidan's anger to show up, but it doesn't. Just another soft smile as he presses his mouth to mine. "You're right. It's not, but loving you is a reason—a really fucking valid one."

Talk about taking an arrow and hitting the bullseye of my heart. I run my fingers along his jaw, feeling the tears once again back up in my eyes. "You broke my heart. I can't risk giving it to you again, no matter how much I want you or how much I've missed you."

With a sigh, Aidan lowers me to the ground, caging me between the wall and his muscled body. "I was a fool, and being away from you taught me a valuable lesson. I want you in my life. I *need* you in my life."

I drop my gaze, unable to meet his intense stare. I've never seen him so riled up with desire. He can barely contain himself, which isn't helping our situation. "No matter how ridiculously attracted to you I am, I think we're better off as friends. That way, our rules don't get in the way, and we don't end up hurting each other again."

A grimace crosses Aidan's face as he taps his hand against the wall. "That's a terrible idea. We are an amazing couple—ask anyone who saw us together. I screwed up—royally—but it's fixable. I'm going to fix us."

How do I argue those words, especially when I've dreamt of

hearing them roll off his tongue? "How do you plan to fix us? We aren't a broken window, Aidan."

"First, I'm going to show you I'm serious about all of it. About *everything*. I'm not running or pushing you away—not anymore. Then, I'll up the ante on the flirtation because let's face it, I know exactly where to touch you to make you quiver." He glides his hand along my hip, his thumb drifting over my clit. "After I've broken your defenses and made you as desperate for me as I am for you, I'll make love to you. All night, every night. I will make it happen. Mark my words."

There is something so sexy about a man taking charge, especially when it involves some delicious, sensual torture.

Especially when it's the man I love more than life itself.

But for now, I'm maintaining my position. If he wants me, he'll have to work for me. "Some pretty heavy declarations, Aidan."

"Maybe, but they're accurate. As for tonight, let's go finish our wine and watch a movie. Then, I'll go home and take a *very* long shower while I jack off and pretend it's actually you sucking my dick."

I giggle at his pained expression. "I am pretty talented in that department."

"Rub it in, please."

"I think that's *your* job tonight."

Just like that, Aidan and I slide back into our flirtatious banter, but I refuse to see it as anything beyond friendly wordplay.

Still, it's far easier to be his friend than his enemy, and that entire family will need my love and care in the coming days. That need trumps any of my personal desires.

We walk to the family room, settling on the couch. Aidan

wraps an arm around me, but he isn't encroaching. He's giving me the space I claimed to need.

"There are two things I need to say."

I bite back a groan, wondering if we're about to take a turn from bad to worse.

"First, I'm playing tomorrow night, and I need you to be there. I've written a new song that you have to hear."

"Okay, I can do that."

"Second, I'm not giving up. Know that. I'm just calling a delay of game for tonight." He leans in, brushing his lips against mine. "I fight for what I want, especially when *I'm* the reason I no longer have it. So, prepare all the arguments you have because I plan to destroy every single one. You're mine, Chloe—plain and simple—but I have no issue proving myself to you. I owe you that but be warned, I'm gunning for you, sweets."

CHAPTER 17
AIDAN

Last night didn't go exactly as planned. I had hoped to swoop in and sweep Chloe into my arms before carrying her to the bed and loving her until she damn well knew my intentions.

Turns out, I've mucked things up more than I care to admit. The pain in her face, when she claimed I broke her heart damn near, broke *me*. In that instant, I saw how much she loved me once and what a bastard I was for tossing something so precious away.

Still, despite everything, Chloe has agreed to come to the bar tonight, and I'm hopeful I can finally prove where my heart lies— with her and *only* her.

Then, I'm making love to that woman for a week straight. I'm serious. We'll only stop to eat and refuel before our next round.

I thought I had it bad before? I'm lost to Chloe, and I never want to be found.

The only quandary with tonight is whether the damn blizzard will hold off until I finish my set. Mother Nature has been generous with the snow this season, and the upcoming storm threatens to dump a foot of the white stuff.

She can dump ten feet, so long as I have Chloe in my arms.

Strolling into the living room, I spy Emily studying the contents of a package. "What do you have there?"

"It's for Chloe," she responds, not bothering to look up.

Taking the package, I shoot my daughter a look of exasperation. "You opened Chloe's mail? Emily, you know better."

"I thought it was for me. It's from some kids named Henry and Jeff. Who are they?"

"I don't know," I reply, although I have a sneaking suspicion they are the boys she helped raise. "Was it a nice letter?"

Emily nods while I gather up the contents of the package. Yay, me, now I get to explain to Chloe why her mail is open—and read—and that I didn't do it.

"They really love and miss her, Dad. They said she was such an excellent teacher, and she always played with them, even when she was tired. Did you know she taught them to read? Chloe also killed all the monsters under their bed. Do I have monsters under my bed?"

I shake my head, but my focus is on the first part of Emily's statement, and I feel my love for Chloe swell exponentially. I'm not surprised she was a good mother to those boys—she has all the attributes of one. She's loving, affectionate, smart, nurturing.

What more could anyone ask for in a mom? Or a wife? Or the love of your life?

"What's that?" Natalie asks, plopping on the couch next to her sister.

"A package for Chloe that Emily opened. It's from the boys she helped raise." I perch on the arm of the chair, knowing I need to broach a very important topic with my kids. "Do you girls miss Chloe?"

"Yes," they reply in stereo.

"She loves you, Dad. I see it in her face. She's loved you for a long time." Natalie cocks her head, shooting me a grin. "You love her, too. Sometimes love makes you do stupid things. That's what Chloe told me, but you always have the opportunity to apologize and start again. You need to apologize for hurting her."

"I have, but I plan on apologizing several more times. I really want Chloe as part of our family."

"Are you going to have another baby?" Emily asks, her eyes wide.

I chuckle, but for the first time, I realize it doesn't sound like a bad idea. It actually sounds like a fabulous one. "If Chloe takes me back, we probably will. You okay with that?"

Emily scrunches her face, considering my question. "Do I have to change diapers?"

"Yes."

"Do I have a choice?"

"No."

"How come Natalie doesn't have to change diapers?" Emily persists, shooting her sister a look.

"Natalie has to change them, too." With a sigh, I run my hand along my jaw. "Girls, we are arguing over a contrived situation."

Emily shrugs, turning on the television. "I like Chloe. I don't like diapers, but I like Chloe more than diapers."

"I'm sure she'll be glad to know that."

Gathering up Chloe's mail, I head for the door.

"Dad?"

"Yes, Emily?" I ask, turning to face her.

She chews her lip, her face pensive. "I guess I can change diapers."

That's my girl. With a smile and a mock salute, I walk out the door.

Seems my kids are on board. Now comes the hard part. Getting Chloe to agree to a future together.

I raise my hand to knock on Chloe's door, but it swings open before I get the chance.

"You're knocking now? How unlike you." She opens the door, allowing me inside.

"Figured I'd try it and see how it felt. I much prefer barging in." I hold out the package. "I apologize. This came for you, and Emily opened it, although I'm not entirely *sure* why she did."

"It's fine. I have no secrets from Emily. Besides, she's too smart for me to even try." Chloe grasps the package, a soft smile coloring her features. "It's from Henry and Jeff. I saw them in New York, and they said they wanted to write to me, but I never thought they would."

"You saw your ex?" Yes, my jealousy is making an appearance. Sue me.

She nods, her focus on the package contents. "I ran into them in a coffee shop. Totally random occurrence."

"I'm surprised he didn't try to win you back, realizing what he lost."

She bites her lower lip, but this time it holds only sadness, not sexiness. "He invited me to dinner, but I declined. Seems my heart belonged to someone else."

A smile stretches my face as I swoop in to steal a soft kiss. "I like hearing that."

"You would," she snaps, but I hear the sarcasm underlying her tone.

Despite everything, the woman hasn't wholly shot down the idea of reconciliation, even if she'd sooner die than admit it.

"You made quite the impression on them."

"I was with those boys every day for five years. They made quite the impression on me, too." Her fingers trace over one of the handmade drawings, and I'm struck by her gentle nature.

For a woman who has spent her life consistently getting the short end of the stick—everyone from her mother to the men she dated—Chloe never *once* faltered in giving her love. That same soft energy I see on her face now is ever-present around my girls. Around Enid. Hell, even around me, and we all know I've made a mess of things.

Something in that moment solidifies my intentions. Whether it's the look in her eyes, that beautiful energy, or just my unabashed love for her, I can't be sure, but I've made my decision.

If anyone deserves to be a mother, it's Chloe, and I'm going to be the man to make her one.

THERE'S QUITE A CROWD IN THE PUB, AND SO FAR, Mother Nature is cooperating. The storm is hung up west of here, but she's crawling steadily in our direction.

Let me woo the woman I love, and it can snow for the next three weeks.

The only hiccup so far? Barbara is here, and she's none too pleased to learn Chloe is back in town. I think she surmised the New Yorker was gone for good when it passed the two-week mark, but if I have anything to do with it, Chloe will become a permanent resident.

"Hi."

I glance up, smiling at Chloe. "Hey, sweets. How are the roads?"

"Not too bad. I came with Enid."

"I'm glad. She needs to get out more. Is Jeff watching the girls?"

"Yes, even though Natalie volunteered. I think that idea freaked Jeff out, and he surmised she wanted to throw a party in the condo, so he's staying with them."

"Smart move. Emily has been known to throw some raucous parties."

"I figured Mia was the one to watch out for."

With a chuckle, I nod in agreement. "That's an understatement. I'll be going on in about ten minutes. Any requests?"

Chloe considers my question. "You have to play Enid's favorite song, obviously, and for me? Sing me something pretty, cowboy."

Leaning in, I steal a kiss from her gorgeous mouth. "That I can do. Something pretty, just for you."

So, I do. We perform several love songs, including a few we haven't played in years. The women seem to love the crooning melodies, but I'm aiming each one at the petite brunette in the back booth.

It's time for our big finale, and judging by the snow falling outside, the timing is perfect.

My nerves kick in as I suck in a deep breath to center myself. It's one thing to perform someone else's love song, but this one is mine. All my thoughts. All my feelings.

All for Chloe.

Go big or go home, right?

I position myself on the stool, guitar in hand. "We're going to end with an original song I wrote last week. I hope you like it. Actually, I hope you love it."

I could have continued with some elaborate dedication, but I believe the song will say all she needs to hear.

I only pray Chloe believes me. Sees how much I need her in my life.

For the *first* time in my life, I question if I'm enough. If I'm somehow worthy of her devotion.

My voice is strong despite my internal fears as I sing the words I penned for the woman I love.

> You're a prayer, a religion, all the reasons I've been given
> And I know you belong with me
> I'm done fighting and denying, you're a life I plan on trying
> From now until the end of me
> You can't see it, but you're the best parts of me
> Life without you isn't the same, and I know that I'm to blame
> Because I let fear overrule my heart
> But if you give me one last chance, I promise my love will last
> From now until the end of me
> A life with you is the only place I ever want to be

THE SONG ENDS WITH A BEAT OF SILENCE BEFORE applause breaks out across the bar, coupled with several whoops of excitement. But I only care what one woman thinks.

Glancing up, I meet Chloe's bright eyes and wide smile. She

blows me a kiss, and I nod toward the back of the bar, desperate to have her in my arms.

The barkeep is closing early, but that's fine by me. The sooner I get my gear packed, the sooner Chloe will be in my arms.

I've just placed my guitar in the case when arms wrap about my waist, hugging me close.

"I guess you approved—" my voice catches when I turn. It isn't Chloe hugging me. It's Barbara. "Barbara, what are you doing back here?"

She tightens her grip, even as I try to back away. "I had to come and tell you what a beautiful song you wrote. I just love it. You are such a romantic."

"Thanks." Is this where I mention I did not write it for her? Extricating her hands from my body, I give them a squeeze. "I have to get out of here. The storm is getting bad."

"Not without a kiss first. I know you had to miss me a *little* bit." Her lips are against mine before I can even process the words.

But my eyes catch one *thing*—Chloe in the doorway, her jaw slack with shock at the sight of our lip lock.

Pushing Barbara off me, I wipe my mouth and race after Chloe.

Fuckety fuck. Come on, universe. Give me a break.

"That wasn't what it looked like."

Chloe spins on her heel, eyes blazing. "Funny, because I think it's *exactly* what it looked like. Only so many ways to play that scenario."

I grasp her arm, desperate to make her listen. "Chloe, please. That kiss meant nothing to me."

"How convenient. It sure as hell meant something to *me*. What is your deal, Aidan? Is your aim to make me look like a fool? Mission accomplished. Here I thought you wrote that song for me—"

"I did. Please believe me. She surprised me back there. That song was for you, not for her. Never for her."

Unfortunately, my beseeching tone isn't reaching Chloe's ears. Not this time. "Actually, she's perfect for you. She has kids. She fits your damn rulebook. Me? I never did. Square peg, round hole, right?"

I pull her to me, feeling her stiffen in my arms. "We fit together perfectly. It just took my feeble brain a while to realize it. But I know now how I feel about you. How I'll *always* feel about you."

She shoves out of my grasp, a tear rolling down her cheek. "I caught you kissing another woman. One who, I'm sure you screwed in my absence. Just leave me alone, Aidan. I don't want to know you anymore."

Twisting around, she dashes out the door and into Enid's waiting car. I know my ex-wife sees me, but she's not abiding by my wishes, either, as she pulls away.

Carrying away the love of my life.

"Shit," I hiss, kicking at a snow pile.

I dash back into the bar, moving at warp speed past Barbara.

"Aidan, what's going on?" she asks, and I turn around, glowering in her direction.

"What's going on? That song was for Chloe. I love her more than I've ever loved any woman, and that was my tribute to her after I screwed up our perfect relationship. But now, she saw us kissing and told me never to speak to her again. *That* is what's going on."

"Aidan, I'm sorry. I didn't know—" Barbara stammers, but I hold up a hand, silencing her.

I don't have the bandwidth to deal with Barbara right now.

Grabbing my phone, I dial Chloe several times, but each one goes straight to voicemail.

"Carl," I bellow, catching my bandmate's eye, "I have to go. I need to get to Chloe."

He nods, a small smile on his mouth. "I'll finish breaking down. Drive safe, man."

With a grateful smile, I rush out the door to my truck.

I have one destination—Chloe's arms—and I won't stop until I'm there.

I PULL INTO MY DRIVEWAY ABOUT FORTY MINUTES later, noting the golden glow emanating from Chloe's windows. At least she's home safe.

Now, I need to toss down my crap and go make things right—for good this time.

Slipping on the walkway, I let out a curse as I open my front door, jumping when I see Enid on the couch. "Are you okay?"

She drums the arm of the couch, her lips pursed in a thin line. "I'm fine, although I can't say the same for Chloe. What happened at the bar?"

Perching on the arm of the chair, I scrub my face with my hands. "Barbara happened. She got the wrong idea after I played that song."

"Does she now have the correct idea?"

I nod, letting out a heated sigh. "She was a bit tipsy, but you know, it's my fault, too. When Chloe left for New York, Barbara stepped in, and even though nothing happened, I allowed the flirtation. A stroke to my ego, right?"

"Did you and Barbara…" Enid motions with her hands, earning a side-eye from me.

"I just told you *nothing* happened."

"Your nothing and my nothing are two different things. Go ahead, keep talking."

"After the show, I motioned to Chloe to join me in the back room. But Barbara got there first and planted one on me. Chloe saw everything and told me she didn't want to speak to me anymore. She wouldn't even let me explain."

"You want my advice?"

"When has my wanting it or not *ever* stopped you from giving it?" It's the truth. Enid has long told me her opinion on things in my life. Why change now?

"I'm only going to say this once. Consider it tough love, from me to you. Give that woman a child. She's amazing, drop-dead gorgeous, smart, and she adores our girls. She also adores you, for some reason or other. Stop screwing up, Aidan. I promise you will regret losing her."

Hopping to my feet, I pace the carpet. "Why do you think I played that song? Hell, why do you think I wrote it? I'm trying to win Chloe back. I tried last night, reassuring her I want what she wants. That I would give her *anything*. She stopped me last night, and after the Barbara debacle, who knows what will happen."

Enid stands, grabbing her coat. "Since when do you let anything stand in the way of what you want?"

"I'm scared, Enid," I admit aloud for the first time. "What if I'm not enough?"

"You're more than enough. You are a wonderful man, and I know you love her."

I nod in agreement. No contesting that statement.

The wind howls against the window, and despite the warmth in the house, I shiver. "You're welcome to stay here. The roads are a mess."

"It's only a couple of miles. I'll be fine. I expect you to be next door within ten minutes."

"Yes, ma'am." After offering Enid a hug, I watch her pull into the snow-laden streets.

My ex-wife is right. Go big or go home.

Time to win the woman who owns my heart.

CHAPTER 18
CHLOE

I collapse against my door, my body sliding to the floor as the tears are finally given their due. Somehow, I held it together for the ride back to my house, namely because Enid doesn't need my petty worries on top of her mammoth issues.

A broken heart is child's play compared to what she's dealing with, even if she knew I was lying when I told her—about forty times—that I was fine.

But Enid opted not to pry. She reads me well, and she knew I wasn't up for speaking about it yet. Perhaps never. Instead, she dropped me in my driveway with a hug and a promise to call and let me know she arrived home safely.

After a few additional moments on the floor, wallowing in my own misery, I stand, the anger overtaking the anguish.

Screw Aidan. He doesn't deserve my tears.

He didn't deserve them when he broke my heart, chiding me for wanting a baby and telling me to settle for a dog.

He didn't deserve them on those lonely New York nights

when I lay in my apartment, missing the feel of his arms around me.

He certainly doesn't deserve them now. Not after I found Barbara's lips attached to his, right after he played a song which I foolishly believed was written for me.

That's the trouble with assumptions—you believe what you want to believe. You can convince yourself of any story, provided it suits your narrative. If you want to believe a man loves you, you will see all the little ways he does. The opposite also holds true.

When I landed in Asheville the other day, I held the belief that Aidan and I were done, a blip in the matrix of relationships. But he appeared to feel the opposite, telling me everything I wanted to hear until my heart, desperate to find a reason to believe him, did just that.

I went to the bar tonight with the idea we would reconcile, and somehow, through a shift in the universe, we might even pursue a future together.

That concept lasted until I walked backstage and found him and Barbara kissing, and I realized that reality and dreams rarely walk hand in hand.

At least Aidan's actions answered one question. The house goes on the market as soon as the blizzard moves out of the area. I'll hire someone else to finish the reading nook because that man will never set foot in here again.

My heart isn't safe anywhere in his vicinity, and for once, I'm putting my needs before my wanton desires.

I'M UPSTAIRS WHEN THE LIGHTS GO OUT. NO SURPRISE, really, considering the storm, but stupid me didn't bother to start the stove when I walked in, and now, I get to muddle through it in the dark.

Good times.

Using the light of my phone, I ease down the steps, noting a human-shaped shadow by the stove.

Either the ghosts in this house are also chilly, or Aidan is here.

The ghosts are more welcome at this point.

I storm toward him, wishing I had that candlestick from the other day to swing at his handsome head. "What are you doing in my house?"

He turns, raising his hands in surrender. "You wouldn't respond to my texts or calls. Did you think I was going to leave it like that? No way, Chloe."

But my temper is running full blast, with every ounce of anger aimed at him. "Breaking and entering is a felony, asshole."

"Then call the cops. I won't resist them."

Releasing a loud groan, I collapse on the couch, noting the ease with which Aidan lights the stove. He's not getting a word of thanks, though. No chance of that happening. "What do you want?"

"I want to fix this, Chloe. Tell you what happened at the bar."

"I saw what happened."

"No, you think you know, and I get it looks bad, but I didn't kiss Barbara. She surprised me backstage, and as soon as I turned around, she planted one on me."

"Am I supposed to believe that?"

"I would hope you would because it's the truth. There are so many things I need to tell you. How screwed up I've been since you left, and how screwed up *that* made me because I wasn't supposed to feel this way. I've never felt this way before."

"Feel *what* way, Aidan? You pushed me away because I didn't fit your stupid rule book. Now, you're screwed up about it? Well, fuck you. You don't get that luxury."

Aidan grabs my arms, pulling me close. "You have every right to be mad. But know this—I'm not walking away again."

"What do you want, Aidan?" I ask, my eyes filling with tears I *swore* I wouldn't shed for him again.

He thumbs my cheeks, his expression soft and tender. "You. I want every facet of you, forever."

No, I can't do this again. There must be a statute on how many times a man can break your heart. "But I'm not what you want, and I don't see there is much else to talk about."

"We have a lifetime of things to discuss, which is good because I plan on spending all my days with you." He reaches into his jacket, tossing a box of candy in my direction. "Random segue, but I was at the store before the gig and saw they had Junior Mints."

I shrug, wondering what drugs this man is smoking if he thinks a box of candy makes a difference. "I'm not forgiving you for a box of Junior Mints."

Aidan chuckles, kneeling by my side. "How about a case of them?"

My only response is a scowl.

He leans in, pressing his forehead against mine, his fingers looped around mine. "I've never been so scared in my life, Chloe, as I was before I played that song. I knew I had one chance to get it right. The right words, the correct approach. It had to be perfect, or it wouldn't work."

I pull back, gazing into his green depths. "What are you talking about?"

"How to make you stay. How to make you want the things I want. How to prove to you I want the things you want."

"But you don't—"

Aidan slides his hands along my jaw, and I feel him trembling. "Will you stop fighting me? At least hear me out. I wrote that song for you. Every word in it is true. You mean everything to me, and I hate you thought, for one second, that you didn't. I said the wrong things. I hurt you. But now I'm trying to say the right things, the things that are in my heart."

"Aidan, we can't—"

"Will you be quiet? Just for a minute, be quiet."

I fall silent, partly because I don't have the energy to fight him anymore. But there's another part of me, albeit a tiny seed, that hopes against hope he means what he says.

A shiver rushes through me, and Aidan shoots me a mock scowl. "Always cold, aren't you?"

"It's freezing in here."

"Let's remedy that," he replies, standing and grabbing blankets and pillows to create a makeshift bed right by the stove hearth. He plops down, holding out his hand to me. "Come here. Before you argue, which I know you excel at, know that it's far warmer here. Plus, you've earned a massage, and you *know* I have talented hands."

"I could also huddle under blankets and take a pain pill." Hey, I'm not making it too easy for the man.

"My way is far more fun."

Damn hormones, they kick rationality's ass every time, and Aidan isn't lying. His hands are incredible.

With a sigh, I slide onto the pile, warming my hands by the stove, all the while maintaining a somewhat safe distance from Aidan.

Apparently, he's not having that, as he scoots closer, sliding his hands under my robe and jerking back when he finds another robe underneath. "How many layers are you wearing? Never mind, the answer is too many. Let's get some of these off."

"It was cold," I retort as he slides my robe down my arms.

"Are you cold now?"

"I will be if you keep stripping off my clothes."

Aidan shoots me a smirk, his 'trust me, you want me to do this' smirk as he pulls my shirt over my head. "I'll warm you up."

"Do I have a say in this?"

He shakes his head, now intent on a new task. Seems since I'm down to my skivvies, he feels obliged to do the same. "You have to lie back and enjoy it. A tragedy, I know, but try to stay the course."

"Why do *you* need to be naked to give me a massage?" I'm not complaining—not really. Aidan's body is a panty-dropping assortment of hard muscles and colorful tattoos. But it's much more difficult to dislike the man when all his gorgeousness is hanging out in front of me.

"I don't need to be naked, but you're cold, so... body heat."

"Clothes also work to keep people warm."

Aidan lays next to me, skimming his hands along the length of my skin. "Not as well, and that's a fact, Ms. Smarty Pants." He tongues a path along the column of my neck, twining his hand in my hair and forcing me to enjoy every second of his affections. "You have the softest skin. Fuck, I missed you, sweets."

"I assume kissing also helps in heat conduction?"

Am I being difficult? Most certainly, but Aidan seems to enjoy my stringent stance.

"It's a bonus. You're getting warmer, aren't you?"

Truth is, my body is damn near implosion point—and Aidan knows it. But there's no way I'm going down without a fight. Sure, he said all the right things these past couple of nights, but he also kicked the crap out of my heart. Staying frosty is my only hope against the heat his lips and hands are generating.

I snatch a corner of the blanket in a sad attempt to shield myself from his sensual onslaught.

"Still chilly?"

Shooting him a snarky look, I shrug. "Maybe you're not as hot as you think you are."

His grin widens. "I hear a challenge, which I gladly accept."

"What challenge is it you think you're hearing?"

"That I can't make you melt... in my mouth." He flits his tongue along the shell of my ear, and I know this is one challenge I'm going to lose—and love every second.

"I think you may be overly confident in your abilities."

"I guess we'll find out."

"Will we?"

Aidan rolls on top of me, pinning my wrists down. "Yes, we most definitely will. Chloe, I've been going crazy these last twenty-four hours knowing you're back. All I wanted to do was barge over here and make you hear me."

"Which is basically what you did both nights."

"I consider them rescue missions."

"How so?"

"I've been a moron, and I wasn't sure how to win you back or if you'd even consider it, but I missed you too much not to try."

"Did you?" Those damn tears show up again, but I blink them away.

"Way more than I care to admit."

Time to make him lay it out on the table—what he wants, what he's offering. "Admit it anyway. Not because I think you owe me for being a shit before I left, but because my heart needs to know the truth."

He sucks in a breath, framing my face with his hands as he presses kisses to my mouth. "I'm in love with you, Chloe. I'm going to make love to you tonight—with nothing between us—

and I'm not going to regret it or question my decision. The *only* bad decision I've made regarding us was to let you leave without knowing how much I need you. How much I love you."

Now it's my turn to tremble. This is the first time Aidan has ever told me he's in love with me. Oh, he intimated something last night, and before I left for New York, I thought he might, but we never said the words to each other. Lord knows I felt the emotion from way back during the early part of our friendship, but I learned from experience that sometimes it's best to keep those thoughts to yourself.

But Aidan's declarations are raw and imbued with emotion. When I meet his emerald gaze—finally—I see the love living there.

Still, the events of the past month haunt me, and I'm not sure I'm ready to tear down the emotional walls I erected during my time alone.

Just because someone says something in the heat of the moment doesn't mean they won't regret it later once they've had time to consider the repercussions.

Aidan skims his hands over my body, littering my skin with kisses. "The smell of you, the feel of you. You're in me, Chloe. I don't want to live this life without you."

I don't stand a chance as the demolition crews invade, tearing down the wall around my heart. I love him too much to *not* give him another chance. Tears fill my eyes as he brushes the hair from my face, smiling down at me. "I missed you, Aidan."

With a heated moan, he claims my mouth. But this kiss screams of ownership. Possession. Where there were boundaries is now assertion. Aidan is staking his claim.

"Let me inside you, sweets. Let me show you how amazing we'll be together." His erection presses against me, his body begging for one more chance to make things right.

But despite any reconciliation, the fear of taking it further toward my original goal holds me hostage. "Maybe we shouldn't. Maybe we should wait."

"Chloe, are you in love with me?"

I can't lie. Besides, I have no desire to lie to Aidan. "You know I am."

His fingers stroke my cheek, and I feel the energy rippling beneath his skin. "I'm in love with you. I got scared. Things were happening so fast. I thought I had my life figured out, but I was wrong. You made me realize how wrong I was."

"I don't want you to end up hating me or regretting this moment."

"I could never hate you. I want to spend the rest of my life loving you. I want us to build a family together. Not yours. Not mine. Ours. What do you say?"

"I'm scared."

"It's okay to be scared, but you're safe. I've got you, sweets. Let me love you."

He slides inside me as soon as I nod my approval, a low moan echoing from us both.

"Holy fuck, you feel amazing, Chloe." There's no doubting the passion etched across his face as he moves inside me.

He feels incredible. We feel incredible together. So right. Pieces of a puzzle that fit, as we were always meant.

Still, that fear hangs by a thread, holding me back from complete surrender.

Aidan pauses, capturing my kiss. "I love you. I want this so much, Chloe. Please believe me."

Those words, that heartfelt sentiment, is enough.

With a cry, I wrap my arms around his neck, allowing the passion to consume me.

Aidan and I move together as one, both whispering words of

love as we brand one another as our own. We are pure heat and fire, pushing each other to a shared release. My hands scratch down his back as my world shatters around me, the feel of him so deep inside me a memory I'll forever keep.

He collapses on me, nuzzling my jawline as our breathing slows. "Best sex of my life. No question."

Running my hand through his hair, I squeal when he nips my palm, a grin splitting my face. I can't help it.

That was incredible, but now, I have to up the ante.

Just for fun.

"We can do better," I counter, earning a wide-eyed look from Aidan.

"Is that another challenge?"

"Depends. Do you accept?"

We taste each other, letting our tongues twine in a leisurely dance, as the fire of passion flames again, our hunger demanding to be fed. "Everything you've got to offer."

CHAPTER 19
AIDAN

I wasn't kidding when I told Chloe I planned on making love to her the entire night. I savored every inch of her body, coaxing orgasm after orgasm until she was spent. Then I slid back inside her and brought her to the edge a few more times.

There is nothing so sexy as a woman who loves sex. With me, specifically.

Hell, there's nothing in this world as sexy as Chloe.

No woman has ever turned me on this way. We're more than a perfect fit. Her body is a prayer to a religion I can't live without, and after taking her raw, I know there is no way I can ever go back.

I don't want to go back. I much prefer moving forward, so long as Chloe is by my side.

Whatever happens, happens.

I'm ready for it.

I'm excited about it.

Bring it on.

When the sun peeks through the blinds, I creep from our makeshift bed, tossing a few logs on the fire before heading to the kitchen. At least the electricity is back on, so coffee *is* an option. The woman wore me out, and judging by her sleeping form, I returned the favor.

In spades.

I also realize, at that moment, how lucky I am to have her in my life. How lucky I am that she gave my sorry ass a second chance.

One thing is certain, I'm never letting her go again.

With a sigh, I step onto the back porch to assess Mother Nature's damage—more than a foot of the white stuff. Thankfully, I bought gas for the snowblower because I'll be needing it today.

Chloe's yard is three times the size of mine. Actually, so is the house. It's a rambler, with six bedrooms and four bathrooms. So much room for one woman.

An idea hits me, then. It *is* a ton of room for one woman. Maybe I can convince her to sell and move next door, or perhaps we can move in here.

Maybe I'm jumping the gun, and the idea of us living together is going to send her screaming into next week.

Still, I don't want to hold back or wait for a perfect time anymore. Now *is* a perfect time. It's all we are promised, and I'm not wasting another minute worrying about inane details.

I know she's talking with a realtor, so I need to broach the topic to ensure her sexy ass is staying down here with me.

That is non-negotiable.

With a last glance at the snow, I step back into the warmth of the house and grab a mug of coffee. As I sit at the table, I see some paper and markers, no doubt purchased by Chloe to play with Mia and Emily.

But I have a different idea.

Just for her.

I put together a breakfast of barely burned toast, jam, and coffee—hey, I never claimed to be a chef—and place it on a tray with a candle and cloth napkin. Under the napkin, I've hidden my secret message for Chloe, a reminder that I meant every word.

Then I return to our campsite, pressing a kiss to the corner of her eye and smiling when she grumbles, tucking herself further into the blanket.

She opens her eyes, blinking up at me, a soft grin on her face. "You're still here."

Tipping up her chin, I steal a kiss. "You're not getting rid of me that easily. Actually, you're not getting rid of me at all."

"I suppose I'll keep you around."

I chuckle, swooping in to nip her neck. God, the way this woman smells. It's incredible. "Have I ever told you how beautiful you are while you sleep?"

"Really?"

"Oh, yeah. Your snore could wake the dead."

With a smack to my chest and without missing a beat, she replies, "Had to do something to cover the sounds of your farting."

God, I love this woman. In actuality, she's a perfect bed buddy and truly divine when she's sleeping.

I could stare at her all day, but it's far more fun to mess with her. Apparently, she has no issue with it.

"I made breakfast."

Those luminous eyes widen. "You did?"

"Okay, it's toast and coffee."

She turns her face up for another kiss as she accepts the tray. "That's perfect because I'm starving."

"Hungry for me or food?" Hey, my cock has been ready for hours, desperate for more rounds with this beauty.

"Let's go with both."

She sits up, taking a mouthful of coffee as she pulls the napkin into her lap. Then she sees it.

My message to her. My reassurance that I'm in it for the long haul.

Her eyes bright with tears, she fingers the piece of paper, a single tear slipping down her cheek. "It was always you." Rising on her knees, she kisses me hard. "It was always us, wasn't it?"

Suddenly, the less than stellar breakfast is forgotten, as I claim something far and away more valuable.

WE SPEND THE DAY TOGETHER, WITH A MAJORITY OF IT naked in bed. The makeshift floor bed was fun as hell, but a mattress wins. Every time.

But it isn't just sexy time between the two of us. We laugh, build snowmen, snuggle in front of the fire.

It's our time, moments that have been too few and far between recently.

On Sunday, I realize the snow will not shovel itself and head out to blow out the walks and driveways. Eventually, we'll have to return to reality, no matter how much I want to stay like this forever.

I'm halfway through Chloe's drive when a strange car pulls in and a woman, totally ill-equipped for the weather, steps out.

Hmm. Maybe this is one of her big-city friends, down for a visit. Her outfit screams money, along with a complete lack of common sense.

It would fit.

"Hi, I'm looking for Chloe Strickland."

Definitely not a friend. She isn't giving off that vibe.

"You found her. Well, she's inside. Can I help you with something?"

"I'm her realtor. I know the weather is terrible, but this house is popular. She's already got offers."

My heart sinks at the woman's words.

I knew Chloe was speaking to a realtor, but this is moving at warp speed, and I haven't talked to Chloe about rearranging our living quarters yet.

Chloe steps onto the porch, her expression curious as she gazes at the woman. "Hi, there."

"Chloe, you are a popular woman. Well, your house is, at least. Five offers, two over asking price."

Her big doe eyes hold mine, and I see the hesitation there. The uncertainty of how I'll respond, if at all.

But the truth is that this isn't my choice. Chloe has to decide she *wants* to stay here in Asheville. I can't tether her to my side or pull a guilt card regarding Enid's illness.

Trust me, I've considered both, but that's beyond unfair.

This is a huge decision—life-changing—and even though we have a fantastic connection, she might not want to step in and play full-time mom to my daughters. She might not want to marry me.

"Five offers? That's... fast," Chloe replies as she chews her lower lip.

"You priced it right, and this is a desirable house. I'll email over the offers, but I was in the area and had to tell you the good news personally. Within a week, you can be free of this house if you so choose."

"Can you give us twenty-four hours, please?" Yes, I'm

jumping into a conversation that doesn't belong to me, but I at least want some breathing room.

Some time to speak to Chloe about her plan.

Our plan.

The realtor shifts her gaze between us before nodding. "Of course. I'll send over the paperwork for you to peruse. Have a good day."

She pulls away, leaving me to stare at the woman I love, not sure what to say to make her stay.

"I only just listed it," she states. "Honestly, I was testing the waters to see if anyone was even interested."

"This is a highly desirable location. Near town with an enormous piece of property. People will want this house." Walking closer, I drum the porch railing with my fingers. "I guess the question is, do you want this house? Do *you* want to stay here?"

Before she can answer, I move to her side, pressing a kiss to her lips.

"Don't feel obligated to answer that right now or to take any of these offers. Sleep on it for twenty-four hours, okay?"

Chloe nods, but there's such an air of uncertainty surrounding her, enough so that it makes me nervous. "I have an article to write, so I'm going to duck upstairs. What would you like for dinner?"

"Actually, I'm headed to Enid and Jeff's house. Family meeting."

"Is everything okay? Relatively speaking?"

"I hope it will be." It's the only reply I can provide as I steal another kiss. "If you need anything, don't hesitate to call me."

She smiles, giving me a flirty wink. "I know, big man. You can run, but you can't hide."

"Where's the fire?" Enid asks, walking into the condo with bags of Chinese takeout.

After leaving Chloe's house, I immediately called my family and demanded an in-person meeting. I need their advice, or at least their opinion on *my* plan.

The last thing I want to do is crash and burn, but I know I need to act and fast.

"Chloe has five offers on her house," I blurt, pacing the rug.

"Wow, I didn't know it was listed." Enid pops open a container of lo mein, sending me a knowing look. "What are you going to do, Aidan?"

Scrubbing my face, I suck in a supportive breath before facing my family. "I have an idea, but I need all of you on board."

My ex-wife's grin widens as she perches on the arm of the chair. "This sounds promising, Mr. Reid. Let's hear it."

CHAPTER 20
CHLOE

With a sigh, I enter the same pub I exited in tears only a couple of nights earlier. Even in my twenties, I never frequented bars this often, but Aidan has a last-minute gig, and he asked me to come and hear him play.

How do I turn down the man I love? Oh yeah, I don't.

I'll admit to having some reservations. After my realtor's unannounced visit, Aidan rushed off to some family meeting, and he still wasn't home by the time I headed to bed.

Then I awoke this morning to a call from Aidan, imploring me to be at the pub at two for an impromptu concert.

The alone time gave me room to consider my options, but I'm no closer to a decision today. There are too many variables: does Aidan *really* want me, does he *really* want a future, what does that future look like?

The list goes on and on.

I don't want to sell my mother's house, but the place is gigantic. If I keep it, I have three options: have about ten empty rooms, start a bed-and-breakfast, or convince Aidan and his girls to move next door.

Unfortunately, the last option requires a third party's approval, and I'm a bit gun shy after the last time.

Still, I must decide, even though I figured the house would sit on the market for a couple of months, giving Aidan and me time to work out a plan... if we end up having a plan at all.

See? Gun shy central.

Stop borrowing trouble, Chloe. You and Aidan are good, better than good.

My brain is right. These last couple of days have been amazing. Aidan has shown me in so many ways that he loves me and wants to be with me.

I need to bite the bullet and sit the man down to discuss Betsey's house.

My house.

Possibly our house, should he agree.

Scanning the interior of the pub, I see Barbara perched at the far end of the bar. Wonderful. I get that she's a local and feels she had a prior claim to Aidan, but I really don't want to be enemies with this woman.

Despite my Yankee upbringing, I want people to like me.

I'd also like to frequent the southern diner and not fear the woman took a piss in my food.

Nodding in her direction, I take a seat on the opposite end, turning my focus to the television. Bowling. All the excitement.

I notice Barbara moving toward me from the corner of my eye and steel myself for the inevitable—and likely uncomfortable—conversation.

"We haven't been properly introduced and, in the south, that's a travesty. Time to break bread... over some whiskey," she states, extending her hand before ordering us both a drink. "I'm Barbara."

Well, this is unexpected.

"Chloe."

"I wanted to speak with you after that unfortunate incident the other night. Aidan and I discussed things earlier and cleared everything up."

Oh crap, what does that even mean? The last discussion they had involved an awful lot of tongue and no words. Forcing out a slow breath, I meet her gaze. "What things?"

She chuckles, but there's no malice in it. In fact, she has a beautiful laugh. She's a beautiful woman. "It's embarrassing to read a situation or person so wrong. Have you ever done that?"

"All the time." Please, God, don't let me be doing that right now. "I think I'm professional level, at this point."

"Deep down, I knew it the first time I saw you two together, and I didn't like it. I didn't like you, even though I had no reason."

"You knew *what* exactly?"

"That Aidan was in love with you and had been since you first arrived."

"Don't know about that," I remark drily, earning a guffaw from Barbara. "He was less than friendly in the beginning."

"You mean the funeral? He was an oaf, but he honestly didn't know the truth about you and Betsey. I did, and I reiterated that fact earlier today."

"You knew Betsey?"

Barbara nods, her eyes glassy. "My own mother was no account, so Betsey took me under her wing. She talked about you all the time."

"Yet she was never around."

"Betsey had flaws, Chloe. Much like us all. Her biggest flaw was sticking her head in the sand instead of facing what she did to you and your father. She wasted years, and she knew it was all on her."

There's something in Barbara's words that brings on a rash of tears. The ability to release some of the anger I've held onto for years. "I needed to hear that, that she was sorry for what she did. I never got to hear it from her. No one thought she was going to die."

"She did," Barbara replies, rubbing my shoulder. "She always had this way of knowing, so she asked me to pass along a message, on the off chance she never got to hug you again. Don't waste a moment on grudges or on what might have been. Betsey always knew you were stronger than her, and she worried that strength might keep you isolated. It's okay to need people, Chloe." She nods toward the stage. "Looks like your man is about to play."

"He's not— "

Barbara stops me with her intense stare. "It's okay to need people, Chloe. Remember that."

"Barbara, thanks for loving my mom."

"That's what I do. Don't worry, you'll be in that group soon, too." With a pat on my hand, she slips away, returning to her date for the evening.

"What was that about?" a voice asks to my right. "Catfight in the parking lot?"

Whipping my head around, my eyes widen at the sight of Enid, Jeff, *and* the girls. "Not hardly, and how are you all here?"

"Kids are allowed during the day. Besides, Mia swore she would keep the drinking to a minimum."

"Good thing, because I can't keep up with her again. She drank me under the table with her juice boxes."

"Hey, you all made it."

I smile up at Aidan, blushing when he steals a kiss—in front of his entire family. "I wondered if you were ever coming over."

"Getting set up. Any requests? Enid?"

"You already know," his ex-wife replies with a grin.

With a final kiss, Aidan strides to the stage while we order a round of drinks and several plates of appetizers.

As always, Aidan's band is on point, regaling us with a festive blend of cover tunes. Before long, the warmth of my friends and the music has soothed my rough edges, allowing me to relax.

That is until Aidan calls out my name. "Chloe, I need you to come here."

Shooting him a look that is part confusion and part terror, I remain rooted to the spot. "Why?"

"Just come here."

"Go," Enid insists, even getting Natalie to give me a slight shove out of the booth.

What happened to female camaraderie and girl power, ladies?

Strolling to the front of the stage, I smile when Aidan drops down next to me, pulling me into his arms.

"Hi, handsome."

"I realized that in the several times we've been out together, I never got a chance to dance with you."

"You're not missing much. I'm not a great dancer."

"I should be the judge of that, though. So, I came up with an idea of when we can dance together."

A nervous laugh bubbles out of my chest. "At least I'm better at dancing than ice skating or billiards, so you should be safe. When is this dancing extravaganza happening?"

"Our wedding."

For a moment, I can't hear anything but my heart thudding in my chest. Gazing into his green eyes, I manage a whisper. "Our what?"

Aidan sinks to one knee in front of the entire bar, which is now completely silent, their gazes aimed toward us. "You're everything, Chloe. From that first lunch together, I knew you were meant for me. I fought it for so long, sure that I knew better. I don't want this life without you. Every moment of this crazy ride, I want to spend by your side. So, what do you say? Marry me?"

He pulls out a small box, and I damn near collapse onto the floor. The proposal floored me. The fact he has a ring, too? When he opens the box, I can't hold back the tears. It's beautiful and classy—a gorgeous round solitaire that catches the light perfectly.

"Before you answer," Aidan continues, a nervous smile on his face, "I have to tell you the rest."

"You don't want me to answer you?" My poor heart, it's beating like a freight train, and I'm entirely unsure how much more it can stand.

"Not yet, because you need to hear everything first and *then* decide. Chloe, I don't really want you to be my second wife."

Oh my God, what is he doing? "You don't?"

He grasps my hands, and I feel him trembling. Glad to know I'm not the only one. "I want you to be my forever one. But there is a non-negotiable condition to this proposal."

I stiffen, wholly uncertain I want to know. Quirking a brow at him, I release a sigh. "Let's hear it."

Aidan frames my face with his hands, but his smile never falters. "It's totally your fault, too, so you *can't* be angry with me."

"No guarantee."

"It's about having a baby."

Great, here we go again.

"You want a baby, right?" Aidan presses.

"I do."

"Well, we can't just have one. They need a sibling."

"They would have siblings. Three of them, actually."

"Our baby would need one close in age. A playmate. Makes sense, right?" His smile widens. "I'm glad we got that settled."

Got what settled?

"Aidan—"

"Don't argue, Chloe. Just say yes and kiss me."

"We're doing this baby thing more than once?"

He considers my statement before nodding. "Yeah. I'm thinking twice."

"Twice."

"You're arguing."

"I'm negotiating."

Laughter rises from the bar patrons, and I can't hold back my smile.

"Are you marrying me or not?" When I stare into his emerald depths, there is such passion there, I fear I might catch on fire and never care that I was burning.

A laugh bubbles out of my chest as I jump into his arms. "Sure."

"I love you."

"You'd better."

I claim Aidan's mouth, feeling him smile against my lips. So, this is what real happiness feels like. The place erupts with applause, but I pull back with a start, realizing it isn't just us in this family unit.

"Wait, what about the girls? What if they're not okay with this decision?"

"Why do you think they're here? Turn around, ask them."

Pivoting, I catch sight of his daughters, all bright with smiles. "Are you okay with me marrying your dad?"

"I still don't want to change diapers, but I love you, Chloe." Emily, just like her father, lays it out there.

"You don't have to change diapers."

"Yes, they do," Aidan interjects, shooting Emily a look. "We talked about this."

"You did?"

Aidan nods, wrapping an arm around me. "When you were gone. I realized even though I could muddle through this world without you, I sure as hell didn't want to. You're my best friend and the love of my life."

"One of, anyway," I reply, more than happy to share that title. "Ditto for you."

"I have a request," Enid interjects, grasping my hand to steal a look at my ring.

"Anything." I mean it, too. I'd move mountains to see Enid smile.

"Make the wedding soon. And please, knock her up already."

"I'm trying," Aidan argues, but his smile never falters.

"I'm sure it's so difficult for you, Aidan," Enid remarks with a wry grin.

"Never said that," he counters, pressing another kiss to my cheek.

Now Enid turns her full attention to me. "I plan on being here for all of it, so get a move on, huh?"

Pulling her into a hug, I let the tears roll down my cheeks. "You're my maid of honor. Kind of have to be there."

Somehow, I know she will be.

A slow song plays over the jukebox, and I turn to my new fiancée, shooting him a cheeky grin as he pulls me into the circle of his arms.

"Is this a practice run?"

"Another day with the only woman I want to spend all my days with," Aidan replies, earning a kiss of approval.

"Thank you."

"For what?"

"Making me stay."

EPILOGUE
AIDAN

"Love is the thread, woven through us all, that ties us together forever. It can't be broken by time, distance, or death, but rather strengthened through the memories that first sewed it together."

These are the words my new wife speaks during our wedding ceremony, and I know there isn't a dry eye in the place.

Chloe is magnificent, beautiful in every facet of the word. But words alone will never do this woman justice.

Her house, or should I say, *our* house, came off the market the day after I dropped to one knee and begged Chloe to be mine. I never asked her to put my name on the deed, but she insisted, claiming if we were building a life together, it would happen *together*.

Then, we made a decision that was as offbeat as the rest of our lives, but somehow, we knew it would work.

The plan was simple. Enid and Jeff would move into my house since the stairs in the condo would be a problem at some point. Besides, this puts Enid near us all day, every day. If she needs anything, we are right there.

As for the girls and me, we moved into Betsey's house, and the girls absolutely adore the fact that it's now *their* home.

It truly feels like home now, and I know it would thrill Betsey that her daughter and friend found love in each other's arms.

We marry in the backyard, on a brisk but bright March day, beneath a pergola I constructed to celebrate the start of our new life.

Good to her word, Enid is the maid of honor, and thankfully, the treatments seem to be holding the devil at bay. Maybe, if we're lucky, we'll get far more than a year.

As our wedding song plays, I twirl Chloe on the floor, pulling her close to me, a permanent grin on my face. "Are you happy?"

"Exceptionally so."

"Happy enough to tell me about that secret you've been keeping?" I steal a kiss, reassuring her I'm not angry. In fact, I'm the complete opposite.

She smacks my chest, a scoff flying from that gorgeous mouth. "How did you know?"

"That's not admitting it. I want to hear you say it."

"Why? You've already figured it out," she counters, saucy as always.

Knitting my hands in her hair, I seize her mouth, not caring that it's hardly a child-appropriate kiss. "Say it, Chloe."

"I'm pregnant."

I often wondered how I would feel if she got pregnant. In that instant, as my heart swells from the news, I have my answer.

"Are you okay, Aidan?"

Picking her up into a bear hug, I squeeze her tight, peppering her face with kisses. "You make my life wonderful. Never forget that I love you. I'll screw up and say the wrong thing, but you are my everything. My heart. My soul. My breath. You make me whole, Chloe."

Her gentle fingers trace the planes of my face, a soft smile coloring her lips. "I was worried since it happened so fast."

"Are you kidding? I figured you were pregnant last month. I must be slacking."

"No," she retorts, patting her stomach, "I think we're good."

"We're more than good. We're perfect."

And we are. So long as she is mine and I am hers, there is nothing we can't handle.

CONNECT WITH M.L. BROOME

Sign up for her newsletter
https://www.mlbroome.com/
BookBub
https://www.bookbub.com/profile/m-l-broome
GoodReads
https://www.goodreads.com/author/show/19088931.M_L_Broome
Facebook
https://www.facebook.com/ML-Broome-350211855703261/
Instagram
https://www.instagram.com/m.l.broome_author/
Amazon Author Page
http://bit.ly/MLBroome

ALSO BY M.L. BROOME

Hook Up (A Driven World Novel)

Reverse Age Gap

Brother's Best Friend

Second Chance Romance

Make You Stay

Friends to Lovers

Single Dad

Opposites Attract

Baby Maker (Cocky Hero Club)

Love After Loss

Second Chance at Love

Emotionally Charged

And Then Came You

Friends to Lovers

Slow Burn

Celebrity Romance

Alchemy Unfolding

Reverse Age Gap

Medical Romance

Ultimate Book Boyfriend

Forgot to Tell You Something
Surprise Pregnancy

Secret Boss

High Angst

A Series of Moments Trilogy Box Set
Celebrity Romance

Love Triangle

Romantic Saga

Yuletide Acres
Holiday Romance

Second-Chance

Single Dad

ABOUT THE AUTHOR

M.L. Broome is a bohemian spirit with a New York edge. She adores dressing up and kicking back, a crisp glass of wine with an equally stunning view, and experiences that make the soul—and mouth—water.

When she's not writing or holding one-sided arguments with her characters (spoiler alert—they always win), she loves losing herself in nature on her North Carolina farm, one of her many rescue buddies at her side.

"Life is beautiful…so are you. Don't forget to look up."

Made in the USA
Middletown, DE
24 August 2021